It was while Patrick Dawlish was at a conference of leaders of the world's police forces, in Zurich, that Felicity Dawlish received the typewritten envelope with an SW1 postmark. The message it contained was very simple: You are going to die. This itself was alarming enough – but the telephone call which followed was even more menacing. For a man with a flat, toneless voice repeated the words . . . and Felicity knew he wasn't joking. Anxiously she awaited Patrick's return . . . only to discover that he had received a similar message. That night their phone rang again. The same toneless voice announced 'You are both going to die' – then the line went dead . . .

D1613255

John Creasey as Gordon Ashe

A Herald of Doom

CORGI BOOKS
A DIVISION OF TRANSWORLD PUBLISHERS LTD

A HERALD OF DOOM

A CORGI BOOK 0 552 10103 6

Originally published in Great Britain by
John Long Limited

PRINTING HISTORY
John Long edition published 1974
Corgi edition published 1976

Corgi Books are published by
Transworld Publishers Ltd.,
Century House, 61–63 Uxbridge Road,
Ealing, London W5 5SA
Made and printed in Great Britain by
Cox & Wyman Ltd., London, Reading and Fakenham

CONTENTS

CHAPTER ONE

'YOU ARE GOING TO DIE'

FELICITY DAWLISH was one of the world's happy people.

There were those who said that, knowing her circumstances and her husband, she most certainly should be happy and there was nothing at all surprising about the fact.

There were others, at least as many, who said that – knowing her circumstances and especially the nature and the profession of her husband – it was astounding that she ever had any peace of mind, still less happiness.

She herself knew what it was like to be frightened. She knew what it was like to live in the fear that the husband, whom she loved, might at any moment be dead or dying from a criminal's hand; that she might never see him alive again. Those who were aware of this were inclined to ask:

'How then can she ever be happy unless her husband is by her side?'

There were a few, much more perceptive, who knew that much though she loved him, her happiness sprang from some deeper source; from within her. As a child she had been happy when another would have been made bad or sad.

Some wanted to know how she could possibly be contented, for she had no children, which was to some a confession of failure in a married woman. Others wondered how she could love her husband so deeply if he had failed to give her children. There was, in fact, no end to the number of questions which people who knew her asked themselves – but they never asked Felicity. Somehow, one didn't pose such questions to her; it would have been like spoiling the dreamlike happiness of a child.

The fact was, however, that Felicity herself knew that she was fundamentally a happy person. The fact that occasionally she had a patch of acute unhappiness not far removed from panic and born out of the fear for her husband did nothing at all to alter the basic characteristic. In any given situation, Felicity Dawlish was more likely to make the best of a situation than bemoan her fate.

'Fate' as a word in the circumstances, would have made her laugh.

On that morning in October she hummed to herself as she scanned the newspapers, partly for the general headlines of news and threats of wars; incidents, disasters, hates, famines and the new pestilence known as 'pollution'; and partly because there might be a reference to her husband. The most likely newspaper to carry a detailed story was *The Times* – *ah!* There it was!

World's Police Debate
New Crime Waves
Zurich – Monday

At the seventeenth conference of leaders of the world's police forces, known to some as the Crime Haters, pessimism was the common factor. Out of the delegates from fifteen nations who addressed the one hundred and one nations represented at the conference on the shores of Lake Zurich today, only one had any improvement to report.

His nation's crime rate is down by 1.05 per cent!

His nation, Kantali, one of the newly-developed nations of Africa, has much on which to congratulate itself. The first three years of its existence saw conditions so bad that such crimes as food robbery, bag-snatching, pocket-picking, were almost taken for granted. An improved economic status and an improved standard of living has brought about an anti-criminous turn for the better – in Kantali.

Not so in the older nations.

The crime rate in the United States of America, according to the then doyen of federal agents, Mr. J. Edgar Hoover, show a leap of 11.5% over last year. In Great Britain the increase is fractionally below nine per cent. In Russia, whose delegate was surprisingly frank about the lawless state of his nation, crime has risen by 7.75% – due almost entirely, of course, to the infiltration of corrupt Western ideas into Moscow and other major cities! France

8

has a rise of 9% and Italy of $7\frac{1}{2}$% although the Police Chief of Milan, representing Italy, admitted that these figures were not final.

Nor was there any great optimism among the distinguished policemen present. Even the Deputy Assistant Commissioner for Crime of the Metropolitan Police Force in London, usually optimistic, found little of encouragement to say. He complained bitterly that the allotment of funds to his own and all delegations was – to quote – 'niggardly'. But cheerful or not he caused the biggest and loudest laugh of the Police Conference when he suggested – tongue in cheek, let it be emphasized, tongue in cheek – that the average citizen might be safe if *he* were locked up in prison cells, allowing the present prison population to walk the streets.

'They would,' declared D.A.C. Dawlish, 'undoubtedly savage one another in one week more than the police can hope to damage them in a year. Instead of complaining about the failure of the police to catch more criminals, our law-makers might be wiser to change the laws which at present give the criminal far more protection than they give the police or the public.'

Felicity looked up from the report, smiling but a little concerned. She could imagine Pat, of course, her great blond giant of a man, standing in front of the audience and saying exactly what he thought. But sometimes he could be too frank. Members of the British Cabinet and Members of Parliament would probably resent those implications very much. Moreover the present Home Secretary – the man in charge of the Home Office which was in turn in charge of police affairs – was a stolid believer in the law as it was, and in senior police officers keeping their mouths shut.

Pat could come home to trouble he had made for himself.

Here in England he seldom gave vent to his true feelings as he must have done in Zurich; he could beat his breast to her, to some of his staff at the Criminal Investigation Department, even to politicians, but usually on a low key. Once overseas, something seemed to explode in him. The Conference, the meeting of the police chiefs from so many countries, created an atmosphere often tense and occasionally eruptive as a volcano. Nothing in this report explained why he had been so vehement, but she knew how tempting any opportunity was.

She scanned the other newspapers, and on the front page of the *Daily Cry*, she found a headline:

British Police Chief
Flays Politicians

On a middle page of the *Globe* was a larger headline and a small photograph of Pat which somehow caught his expression; half-whimsical and with a touch of defiance. This headline screeched:

Dawlish Damns Law

'Oh, Pat, Pat,' Felicity cried aloud.

She found smaller paragraphs, not so sensational, in the other newspapers which the Dawlishes had delivered daily. Then she went out of the kitchen where she had been reading as she drank coffee, into the big room beyond. This was a penthouse at the top of a tall modern office building on the north bank of the Thames not far from Lambeth Bridge, and consequently it had a magnificent panoramic view from two walls which were almost all glass. In the distance the skyline was dominated by the dome of St. Paul's, with the spires of many churches and even the four towers of the Tower of London to add to the beauty. The river wound away in each direction, making its great loops, and startlingly close to her was Big Ben and the impressive Gothic pile of the Houses of Parliament. From one window was a view of Whitehall with its old buildings, the Cenotaph with its simple tribute to the millions of dead of two world wars and, beyond, Nelson atop his column, lord of all he surveyed.

She saw none of these things.

She saw only the turrets of an old building close to the Embankment and the northern approach to Westminster Bridge; turrets of the 'old' New Scotland Yard. When the headquarters of the Metropolitan Police had been moved to the new premises off Victoria Street, Dawlish's section of the C.I.D. had been left on the top floor of the old.

Sometimes, she could almost imagine that Pat was at one of the windows, waving to her.

But not now. He was at the morning session of the conference at Zurich, oblivious of the mountains and the great blue lake and the countless small yachts moored to buoys or else moving gently in a soft breeze. When he was with the Crime Haters he was the most single-minded man in the world.

Today was the last day of the meeting in Zurich.

She heard a ring at the front door; two long blasts. That would be the postman, and it meant that he had a registered letter or a packet so bulky that it wouldn't go through the letter box. She went to open the door, but it wasn't the post-man, it was a telegraph boy in a blue uniform, wearing a crash helmet.

'Telegram for *Mrs.* Dawlish, ma'am.'

'I'm Mrs. Dawlish,' Felicity said.

'Thank you, ma'am.' The youth handed her the buff-coloured envelope and went off, but before he could enter the lift nearby he stood aside for the postman and for the Dawlishes' 'daily'. Felicity never saw the 'daily' help without feeling bewildered, and even baffled. Why *should* one of the most attractive young women she had ever seen choose to do such a job?

There was a large bundle of letters, which a youthful, long-faced, sparse-bearded postman thrust into her hand with a melancholy:

'Good morning.'

'Good morning,' Felicity said, letters in one hand, tele-gram in the other.

'*Good* morning,' Lois Kenning had a wicked gleam in her lovely dark eyes. She was in her middle twenties with a face and figure which could turn most men's heads. 'All your blessings have come at once.' She closed the door and allowed Felicity to move across the passage and into the big room. Then with the same wicked tone in her voice she went on: 'The master's been having himself quite a time in Switzer-land, hasn't he?'

'So you've read the newspapers!'

'The *Mirror* was magnificent,' declared Lois. 'It said the Prime Minister should make the master Supremo of the Politzia.'

'Oh, my goodness,' exclaimed Felicity. The *Mirror* was one newspaper they didn't have delivered. 'Did you bring your copy?'

'I left mine for my dear, delightful, deluded husband,'

replied Lois, 'but I bought another – I may charge it to housekeeping, mayn't I?' Her expression changed as she looked at Felicity's right hand, and she went on contritely: 'Oh, I am a beast. One day I'll make you so exasperated that you'll throw me out, and you'll be wholly justified. Shouldn't you look at the telegram?'

'I'd almost forgotten it,' Felicity declared. She put the letters on the arm of a huge couch and slit open the telegram envelope; it tore with jagged edges.

Lois hovered.

Felicity glanced down:

Sweetheart, began the telegram, and her heart leapt. *Pay no attention to the newspapers and if anyone telephones you for comment please don't. Conference going very well organizationally despite the gloom of percentages. Who was it said that figures can prove everything? Zurich is as lovely as ever – all that's missing is you.*

The signature was simply: *Pat.*

Lois murmured: 'All's well I can see,' and moved towards the kitchen which could be entered both from this big room and from the passage. Felicity heard but didn't really notice what she had said. *All that's missing is you.* She had no doubt at all that Pat meant it; that he could enjoy life tremendously when away from her yet constantly miss her.

She read the telegram again more slowly so as to relish it to the full, and had just finished when the telephone bell rang. She moved to the far end of the couch and lifted the receiver.

'Felicity Dawlish.'

'Mrs. Dawlish, this is Anderson of the *Daily Globe*,' a man said quietly. 'I wonder if you would be good enough to tell me whether you agree with what your husband said in Zurich last night.'

'I don't know what he said,' replied Felicity promptly.

'He said that—' Anderson began suavely.

'You really wouldn't expect me to comment on a comment, would you?' Felicity asked, sweetly.

Anderson laughed, and said: 'He really is a remarkable man, isn't he?'

'With that I fully agree,' Felicity conceded. 'You may even quote me.'

'Do you agree with his general feeling about the rising crime rate?' asked Anderson.

'Is there such a thing?' asked Felicity.

Anderson laughed again: 'I should have known better than to try to get any comment from you! Mrs. Dawlish, do you worry much about your husband?'

'About what he says? Never! About the danger he shares with any policeman anywhere in the world? Often,' Felicity replied.

She soon rang off and opened the first letter, from a cousin of Pat. She opened the second and the telephone bell rang again: this time, it was the *Daily Cry*. She gave the caller less time even than Anderson, and read two more letters: an invitation to a party and an invitation to join a committee for relief work in one of the new African states. The third newspaper telephone call came then, this time a woman. By now Felicity realized just how much notice was being taken of the outburst in Zurich, and if the Press were following that up so zealously she could be sure that the politicians and civil servants concerned were at least alive to it.

For a while, at least, there was a respite in the telephone calls.

She had only one letter left to read, a typewritten envelope with, she noticed almost mechanically, a *London S.W.1* postmark. It was stuck down very firmly, and she had to get a paper knife from an escritoire in a corner before she could get it open. She took out a sheet of paper folded very tightly and with at least one fold too many, so that it was quite difficult to smooth out. She had it nearly open when Lois appeared at the kitchen door.

'Lunching in or out?' she inquired.

'I'll be in today,' Felicity replied, absently.

'Do devilled eggs sound about right?'

'Lovely,' Felicity answered, and at last had the sheet of paper smoothed and easy to read. Lois had gone back into the kitchen and this room high above London was very quiet as Felicity read a typewritten sentence:

You are going to die.

That was all: just the five words, as plain and direct as words could be.

CHAPTER TWO

ANGER IN HIGH PLACES

At first, the sentence did not really sink in. Felicity read it again, just the single sentence in the middle of the page; the sentence itself had not been touched by the creases where the paper had been folded. She read it two or three more times until it caught up with a delayed shock effect. She felt as if someone had kicked her in the stomach. A wave of nausea made her stagger towards the couch, and a heavy weight seemed to have descended on her breast.

In the next room, Lois was singing:

'*To dream the impossible dream, tra-la, to do-dee do-da-do-de dah.*' The door opened again and she came in, lovely hair tucked under a dust-cap, a plastic box containing a polish and cleaning cloths for the windows swinging in front of her. '*To fight the invisible foe!* I never can remember just how that goes. You did say "windows" this morning, didn't you?'

She stopped short.

Felicity tried to look unconcerned but it simply wasn't possible. The five words now hovered in front of her eyes as if written on the very air, and seemed to cut Lois's face in two.

You are going to die.

'Mrs. Dawlish,' Lois said. 'What's happened?' She put the box down on a chair and moved across quickly. 'Oh, my dear, what is it? Your husband isn't hurt, is he?'

Felicity shook her head.

The younger woman was suddenly on her knees in front of her, taking her hands, looking up into her face.

'Please tell me what it is. If I can help—'

'It—' Felicity began, her voice a croak – 'it's nothing.'

'Oh, I can see it's absolutely nothing at all,' scoffed Lois, squeezing her hands. 'I can be relied on not to talk, really.' Her eyes were a lovely, shiny brown – the colour and brightness of a chestnut just taken from its spiky green husk.

Felicity gulped, and touched the letter; if that single sentence could be called a letter. Lois turned it round in her lap, took the words in at a glance, and looked up quickly still full of concern.

'What a beastly thing to happen!'

'I can't – I can't imagine why it's affected me so much,' Felicity said, her voice less hoarse. 'It's not exactly the first threat I've ever had.'

'But it's so – so cold-blooded,' stated Lois, with sharp perception. 'Just out of the blue, like that. I'd like to choke the life out of anyone who would do such a thing, especially to such a darling as you.' She squeezed Felicity's hand more tightly. 'Do you know I think you're quite the nicest woman I've ever met.'

'Oh, nonsense!'

'It isn't nonsense, and I am not given to making extravagant statements.' The younger woman smiled up into Felicity's face and went on: 'In fact you're the dearest dear and *that's* damnable.' She tapped the paper vigorously. 'Like a cup of tea?' Without letting go of Felicity's hands she got to her feet and then pulled at Felicity so that she either had to get up or resist; and she did not feel like resisting.

The paper fell to the couch.

'Shouldn't you tell your husband's office or something?' asked Lois.

'I suppose I should,' admitted Felicity, 'but a few minutes won't make any difference. And I'm not really sure I should take it so seriously.' They went into the kitchen, which was bright and spotless and where a kettle whispered gently on a low gas. 'After all, we *all* are.'

'Are going to die, you mean?'

'Yes.'

'We don't have to be reminded of it like that,' said Lois, briskly. She turned the gas up under the kettle, and took cups and saucers out of a dresser with sliding glass doors and put them on a tray, took milk from a tall, white refrigerator and sugar from the larder. 'It always baffles me that we women haven't found a short cut to making tea, I think it's a masculine plot to keep us so busy in the kitchen we never really have time to think.'

She was talking to keep her, Felicity's, mind off the note, of course. In many women that would have irritated her, but

Lois Kenning carried it off with an insouciance which made it acceptable. Soon, the tea was made and brewing, and Felicity was sitting on a stool on one side of the breakfast bar and Lois on the other. In moments like these Felicity realized she was at least half-a-head taller than the other woman.

'You *did* say it isn't exactly the first threat you've had, didn't you?'

'Yes.'

'Have you really had a lot?'

Felicity, feeling much better, put laughter in her voice as she answered: 'Oh, hundreds!'

'No, seriously.'

'Dozens,' Felicity compromised.

Lois frowned; a drawing together of her brow and her eyes in a curiously attractive way.

'Really?'

'Seriously.'

'So dear demanding David wasn't so deluded after all.' Lois began to pour out the tea, and hitched herself up on a bar stool as Felicity did the same. '*Dozens.*'

David was her husband, to whom she referred fairly frequently in an affectionate form of alliteration and derision. Felicity had never seen him, only once seen a photograph or more truly a drawing, and understood from something Lois had said that he was an artist.

The tea was stinging hot; just right for her mood.

'I don't see where your David comes in,' she remarked. 'What was he deluded about?'

'Danger,' Lois replied.

'*Danger?*'

'Yes, in working for you. In one way he didn't want me to, although in another he thought it was a wow.'

'Goodness,' Felicity said, startled. 'Why shouldn't you work for me?'

'According to David some men attract trouble and your husband is one of them, and other men make trouble by going headlong into it and your husband is one of them, too, and where a man is trouble-prone – only David said danger-prone – his wife is sure to be on the receiving end sometimes and anyone who works for the wife might become involved.'

Lois stopped, almost breathless, and sipped her tea. But she did not look away from Felicity, who was beginning to realize what attracted her about this girl: you could never be sure what she would say or do next, and she had a most becoming matter-of-factness.

'Well, he wasn't wrong,' Felicity observed.

'No.'

'But what made him so sure?'

'He is the world's most prodigious reader of newspapers,' answered Lois. 'He said he can remember Patrick Dawlish being in the newspapers ever since he was six. Or it may have been seven. He has a tremendous admiration for your husband, don't misunderstand me – it's just that he wanted me to know there was a danger of becoming involved.'

'And yet you took the risk.'

'Well, David isn't always right,' said Lois practically. 'I wanted a job which wasn't too exhausting and where I didn't have to fend off romantic young men or hopeful old ones all the time. And I'm not really qualified to do anything but housework or sell groceries and the like over the counter. And I *loved* the view from these windows the moment I first came here, after I'd answered your advertisement. Took to you, too,' she added brightly: and actually laughed. 'Honestly, I did!'

Spontaneously, Felicity pressed her hand.

'I couldn't believe that anyone under sixty would really want this job and be able to do it,' she remarked. 'How long have you been here now?'

'Three weeks.'

'Good weeks, too,' Felicity said with feeling. 'And you are the first house help I've had whom Pat doesn't want to shoo away the moment he's home.'

Solemnly, but with her eyes glowing, Lois said: 'I usually get along with men.'

Felicity found herself laughing, and the effect of the note was already almost gone. She had no idea how long she would have stayed talking to Lois had the telephone bell not rung. She looked at the extension in the kitchen without favour, thinking it was probably another newspaperman.

'Shall I say you're out?' asked Lois.

'No, I'll talk to whoever it is,' said Felicity, and she took the receiver. 'This is Felicity Dawlish.'

'Good morning, Mrs. Dawlish,' said a man with a clear and familiar voice. 'This is Gordon Scott.'

'Good morning, Gordon.'

The caller was Chief Inspector Scott, and second-in-command at the London headquarters, a youngish man whom she had come to know well and to trust and whom Pat both liked, respected and trusted. He did not make a habit of calling without good reason, and she wondered fleetingly whether his call could have anything to do with the cryptic note she had received.

Nothing in his voice suggested that kind of trouble.

'Do you happen to know what time the D.A.C. is coming back?' he asked.

'Not the slightest. Have you?'

'No,' answered Scott, promptly. 'I thought it just possible after the furore caused by his speech last night that he might come straight to you. I don't want to alarm you, but – er—'

Gordon obviously did not know how to say just what he wanted to say, but experience with him had told Felicity that it was better to let him talk on at his own speed rather than to interrupt him. So she waited, but her heart dropped.

'One or two of the top brass at the Home Office and one or two Members of Parliament have taken a dim view,' Gordon went on at last. 'And the Commissioner has left word for Mr. Dawlish to report straight to him as soon as he gets back.'

'So they're after his blood already,' Felicity remarked, her voice touched with bitterness.

'The thing is,' went on Gordon Scott earnestly, 'I thought if he got in touch with you, you might head him off the office. At least he could have a night's rest before having to cope. I'm calling from my flat, so that no one can overhear.'

'If he gets in touch with me, I'll tell him,' promised Felicity, but she found herself laughing. 'He may feel like knocking some heads together, of course.'

'I know. That's what I'm afraid of,' replied Gordon Scott ruefully. 'I – er – I don't think this should be taken lightly, it's not a thing he can breeze through, I'm afraid. That's my considered opinion.'

'I'll tell him that, too,' Felicity said, more soberly. 'Thank you, Gordon.'

She rang off, knowing he was troubled both by the situation and by what he had said.

Lois had disappeared; she showed a nice understanding of when she should linger and when she should leave Felicity alone. Felicity crossed to the sink and the window which had a panoramic view over another part of London, mostly the west side and suburbs. She could see Buckingham Palace and Westminster Cathedral, the Hyde, Green and St. James's Parks and the new buildings near them, and against the sky-line, and yet she was hardly aware of them. Gordon Scott had not told her everything, of course; simply enough to make sure she tried to persuade Pat to take this seriously. And the fact that he had gone to his flat to telephone rather than risk being overheard in his office spoke volumes.

The top brass was taking Pat's outburst very seriously indeed; in fact, taking a most disapproving view.

She went into the big L-shaped room with the foot of the L near the kitchen and dining alcove, the other with those wonderful windows facing north and east. She ignored the five-word note on the couch and picked up the telegram. The key words were:

Pay no attention to the newspapers, and if anyone tele-phones you for comment please don't.

She had assumed that he had expected the newspapers to call her, as indeed they had, but she now wondered if he had expected repercussions from the Powers That Be and had indirectly prepared her for that as well as the Press.

If he hadn't, Gordon Scott certainly had!

Lois was on the far side of the room, cleaning the windows with a thoroughness which suggested she actually enjoyed the physical activity: and these windows were huge. Spray on *Windowcleer*, allow to dry, polish ... Spray on *Window-cleer*, allow to dry, polish. She was working to a rhythm and did not look round although she almost certainly knew that Felicity was in the room.

Felicity went out by the passage door.

Off the passage were the bedrooms, two to the right, one to the left, each with its own bathroom, as well as a cloak-room and two boxrooms. At times too large for them it was nevertheless a dream of a flat, and she loved it. She was away with Pat a great deal, often out in London on goodwill com-mittee work, spent a week now and again in Scotland with her ageing mother, and had never really had satisfactory help in running the flat.

If only Lois would continue to like the job.

The talk about David and his misgivings had given her a sense of uneasiness but it was no use worrying. In any case this would not go on for ever, a young married woman would almost certainly have a baby before long, and no matter what the protestations no girl could run her own home, look after a baby and spend six hours a day looking after someone else's domestic affairs. She told herself to put Lois out of her mind but only succeeded in letting anxiety about Pat come in.

She wished she knew why Gordon Scott had been so concerned. He must have a very strong reason for talking as he had.

Should she telephone Pat, in Zurich?

The question was no sooner in her mind than out of it. He would be extremely busy with the conference, of which he was vice-chairman, and the preoccupations with the job in hand were as much as any man could reasonably carry. Moreover, this was a particularly important conference. A few months ago it had been decided that the permanent headquarters of the conference should be in the small African state of Kantali. A secretariat had been selected, and was being put to the test for the first time. On such occasions Pat was inevitably needed; he knew more about the conference than anyone else except a Dutch policeman, van Woelden, and both men would be stretched to their limits.

It was a thousand pities, too, that the note struck at Zurich had to be such a depressing one: even in his telegram he had mentioned the mood of depression. Suddenly, she decided what to do, and her heart lifted. She sat at her writing bureau in the big bedroom and wrote in cable form:

> *Bless you for your telegram. Have one comment I want to discuss before you see anyone else so please come straight home and telephone me when to expect you – Felicity.*

That would bring him!

She sent it off by telephone, feeling much lighter-hearted, and realizing that was due at least in part to the fact that he would be home tonight. There was no change in the situation, just in her mood. When the telephone rang she plucked it up and announced with a lilt in her voice:

'This is Felicity Dawlish.'

A man with a flat, toneless voice uttered just five words:

'You are going to die.'

CHAPTER THREE

APPLAUSE

DAWLISH sat down on his chair on the raised platform at
the end of the big conference room.

He had made a few announcements about the next
session, which would be in Buenos Aires; it fell to him, as
vice-chairman of this conference, to cope with some of the
formalities. Hanlo, Chief of the Swiss Police, was in the chair,
a small man who had presided with distinction but committed
himself to no opinions; characteristic, Dawlish had long
since learned, of the police of some of the smaller nations
whose crime problems were less extensive than those of the
larger countries.

The conference room, built on a pier which reached a
hundred yards into Lake Zurich, was large enough for five
hundred people, but by a cunning arrangement of drapes
and of concertina type doors, it could be made to appear
comfortably full no matter how many people were present.

Give or take a few, there were two hundred and ten present at this meeting.

The room was of simple design, with wooden beams and
walls and on one side, huge windows which faced south and
so admitted the bright sunlight. The ventilation system was
so good that even without air conditioning the room was
pleasantly cool. From this window and one, smaller, on the
other side the picture-blue of the lake showed with the tops
of the sails of countless yachts; and in the distance, the hills
which led, not far away, to the great mountain.

In the split-second which he took to sit down on an angu-
lar-looking but comfortable chair, Dawlish marvelled again
at this meeting and the men (with a few women) who made
it up. In a single sweep he could see here in Zurich, Switzerland, several Japanese and Australians, Brazilians and
Koreans, Vietnamese and Chinese, Egyptians, Kenyans and

men from the emergent African States (all of them black), Americans and South Americans. Many he had seen before, some were new to the conference, and today more nations were represented here than ever before.

There were Russians and West Germans; Finns and Bolivians; Canadians and New Zealanders – there were police chiefs from nearly every police force in the world, drawn together because crime was no longer solely a national business; could no longer be handled with full effectiveness within a city or a country but spread far and wide throughout the earth.

Drugs grown in Turkey were a threat to society in fifty countries, some of them half the world away.

Jewels stolen from London could be on offer for sale in Tokyo in forty-eight hours, or even less.

Murderers could commit their crimes and be out of the jurisdiction of the police where they had killed before the bodies were discovered.

Smuggling of every kind and of every conceivable commodity, from furs to furniture, heroin to tobacco, diamonds to industrial formulae, had become as much a part of the world's society as pollution and the population explosion and war.

The police of the world had been slow to see the need for a system of co-operation and communication; a system and a clearing house for crime and news about crime which would serve the world as Scotland Yard served London, and the Federal Bureau of Investigation served the United States and the Sûreté Nationale served France. Interpol had been partly effective and still was, but the greatest need was for this organization, still labelled the International Police Conference and still known popularly as the Crime Haters.

It was becoming more and more effective as a body.

But crime was on the increase all the time, and the International Police Conference had not the funds nor yet the authority to do all it could and should. This had been the main burden of many of the speeches; delegate after delegate had spoken into microphones – which had instant translation into French, English and Japanese whatever language used by the speaker – of the unreadiness of many governments and civil servants to pay reasonably for and to give full aid to the organization.

Last evening, Dawlish had summed up these speeches with a fire which was rare at such meetings; summed up and joined in the widely felt plea.

Last evening he and a few others had discussed that main problem as well as the problems of organization. The simple truth was that without more funds they could not pay for a fully equipped secretariat. Hopes which had been raised sky-high after one of the greatest successes the organization had achieved, had gradually faded. Promises of support made in good faith by representatives of governments had not been carried out: politicians when assessing budgets were the least emotional of human beings.

Much of this went through his mind as he sat down after the morning's remarks.

He did not quite understand what followed. There was a burst of applause which came spontaneously from several parts of the room, more than the polite clapping which his announcements had warranted. The applause grew. One moment half-a-dozen men here and half-a-dozen there were clapping: the next all of the two hundred joined in, and those who had started stood up and clapped with even greater fervour. Dawlish placed his hands on the arms of his chair and stared unbelievingly.

Why should they behave like this?

The woman sitting below the platform and on one side, Camilla Felista, sprang up and joined in, facing him. She was from a small state in South America, one of the most remarkable women he had ever known, with a mind like a computer; as the secretary of the organization she could not be bettered.

She seemed to go wild with enthusiasm.

As Dawlish looked about him in complete bewilderment, Hanlo stood up, joined in the clapping and after a while raised his arms so that the applause began to fade. When there was sufficient quiet, he said dryly:

'Our vice-chairman is a most remarkable man. He appears to be genuinely puzzled. He must be the only one in this auditorium who does not know that his outspoken statement last evening summarized what all of us feel, although we did not realize its full significance at the meeting. It is indeed time this organization ceased to be the Cinderella of the police of the world.'

The applause burst forth again, and Dawlish simply threw up his hands as if in surrender.

But soon, the mood quietened and the session closed.

The delegates had made plans to reach the airport quickly, very few would stay in Zurich overnight. The hotel opposite the pier where the conference had been held echoed to good-byes in dozens of languages, and even Dawlish's powerful hand began to ache from constant shaking. He stood with Hanlo in the foyer, perhaps an inch taller than the Swiss, who was a very tall man, vast across the shoulders and deep in the chest.

At last, all were gone; even the newspapermen and the photographers.

Camilla Felista came out of the room which had been turned into a conference office, a large woman with untidy but attractive grey hair, big irregular features which some-how conveyed a sense of bursting vitality. She had two or three letters in her hand, and when she drew closer Dawlish saw that one was a cable, the other a typewritten envelope. And both were for him.

'I am angry in the extreme,' Camilla declared, her eyes flashing. 'The telegram was kept in the hotel reception office, only by chance did I find it. The letter was by the latest post.'

Dawlish opened the telegram, and his expression relaxed when he read it. He handed it to Hanlo, who read and smiled dryly, making only one remark:

'So your wife has not been free from the Press.'

'I wouldn't expect her to be left alone.' Dawlish, who had some kind of idea what he would run into when back in England, began to open the letter. It was stuck down very firmly and he took out his penknife to slit open the envelope. The letter was folded several times and was smaller than need be for the size of the envelope, which was type-written.

At last he opened it.

He read: *'You are going to die.'*

The five words took Dawlish completely by surprise.

Had he had the slightest warning he would have kept a poker face. As it was, his expression changed ludicrously so that Hanlo and Camilla could not fail to see that something was wrong.

'What on earth has happened?' Camilla cried.

Dawlish gulped, read again, then turned the note so that each of them could read it. He heard Camilla's outraged comments and saw Hanlo go pale; it occurred to him then that each took this cryptic note exactly as he had: with the utmost seriousness. He looked at the envelope, and saw that it was postmarked *London, S.W.1,* and was date-stamped the day before yesterday.

'Shall I have the envelope checked for fingerprints?' asked Hanlo.

Dawlish said at once: 'Will you?' He knew that the Swiss would not take long, and added: 'If you could get a message to me at the airport, I'd be grateful.'

'That shall be done,' promised Hanlo.

'It is the outrage!' Camilla declared. 'Who would threaten such a man as you, Mr. Dawlish? It is the most wicked thing.'

He did not tell her so but there were dozens, possibly hundreds of people who would gladly see him dead. There were at least four different organizations, including the Mafia, which had not the slightest desire to see the Crime Haters become stronger and would gladly cut down one of its leading lights. The trouble with a note like this was that it gave no clue as to the sender. It could even have come from someone who was mentally disturbed.

He wished he had not shown how much it had affected him, and then found himself wondering why it had hit him so hard. It might simply be some crank, someone who wanted to harass him. And he had been in a curiously exalted frame of mind after that burst of applause, so preoccupied with the problems of the Crime Haters, that he had been taken completely off his guard.

Hanlo said: 'I hope you find the sender of the letter quickly, Pat. And I hope you can persuade your officials in London that you are right about our needs. I shall make that very clear to my government.'

And Dawlish had thought he was sitting on the fence!

Hanlo went off, after more formal leave-taking. Dawlish followed Camilla into the office which she had organized with remarkable efficiency; she could do the work of ten. Hanlo would be at hand to help her with the final clearing up.

'And when it's done you must come to London for a few days,' Dawlish said.

Her eyes lit up; even recollection of the five-word message did not seem to worry her now.

'To see Scotland Yard,' she breathed. 'It is a life dream!'

She was talking about this and the wickedness of the writer of the message when a police car arrived to take Dawlish to the airport. It was then half past seven. Camilla was asking if there was anything she could do for him, and as they walked towards the car, he said:

'Will you telephone my wife and tell her what flight I am on? Ask her not to meet me but say I will go straight home.'

'This will be a pleasure,' Camilla said warmly.

He stepped into the car.

Beyond was the great expanse of the lake, and the line of mountains, dark against the sky which was already losing its brilliance. And in front of him was the pier and the conference halls. Several people were on the pier, several men loitering about it.

Loitering.

Dawlish found himself wondering if one of them would attack him.

As he said good-bye to Camilla who seemed to be in tears, he wondered if a stranger on the steps of the hotel was an assassin.

As the police car drove off, he wondered if it were being followed.

The simple, inescapable fact was that the words of the note had put him more on edge than he had been for a long, long time. And he remained uneasy as he went through immigration and then through customs, mere formalities in each case since his identity was well known, and then walked from the gate towards the aircraft.

There were so many strangers about; wherever one looked. Even one of the men in uniform might be a would-be assassin.

What the hell was the matter with him? he asked himself savagely. Why should he be so affected? He had received threatening letters phrased brutally enough to make his blood run cold, and they had never affected him like this.

27

Perhaps the stark simplicity of these five words explained their effect; that, added to the timing.

There were only two empty seats in the first-class of a *Swissair 707*, and the economy class seemed crowded. He was one of the last on board and almost at once the aircraft began taxiing to the runway. Unless by some freak of chance the writer of that note was on board, he was completely safe until they reached London Airport. This was an ordinary passenger flight and it would be easy enough to find out who had booked for it. For that matter there could be a bomb in the baggage hold—

He thrust the thought aside.

There wasn't even the slightest reason to suspect danger from anyone on board, no reason to expect trouble in London. He could unwind with Felicity. That was what he needed, a period of unwinding, and Felicity was perfect to help in the process, except . . .

He didn't want to tell her about the note: did not want to scare her.

As he pondered, drank a whisky and soda brought by a stewardess with surprisingly thick but well-shaped legs, he thought of the odds against keeping the 'scare' away from his wife. They weren't very good! She had grown so accustomed to his moods that she was like an extension of himself; and she would soon sense that he was troubled.

It would be good to see her.

And they would dine at home with a meal prepared by Lois Whatever-her-name-was, a pleasure on the eyes, and cooked by Felicity – unless Felicity prevailed on the younger woman to see the whole meal through.

He looked out over the Alps and for a few moments, was lost in wonder at their snow-tipped grandeur. When they were behind him, he dozed. Whenever he woke from the doze, he was still wondering whether to tell Felicity about the scare message, or let news of the note ride for the evening.

At that time, Felicity was thinking: But I can't tell him as soon as he gets back. It doesn't matter how scared I am.

And she *was* scared.

The letter itself had been quite bad enough without the telephone call, and now every time the telephone bell rang she wondered if it would be the caller with the toneless voice. Even recollection of that made her shudder. When it rang a little after six o'clock, however, it was the South American woman Dawlish had told her about, and the woman's voice sounded warm and eager and reassuring.

At last, Felicity put down the receiver.

The aircraft was due to land at London at 7.22, and Pat should be home by eight o'clock. If he wasn't here by eight-fifteen, she knew she would begin to worry.

CHAPTER FOUR

ON TIME

AT eight o'clock, Felicity *did* begin to worry. She knew it was absurd but there was nothing she could do about it. Lois had put a piece of sirloin in the oven and some peeled potatoes in the sizzling fat around the joint; the vegetables were prepared, brussels sprouts and runner beans, everything was standing by and all she had to do was put these on and make the rich, glutinous gravy which Pat liked. She wore a loose-weave suit, autumn brown in colour, beautifully cut, and an off-white blouse. She knew she looked as well as she could. By the stove was a small apron for use while she finished cooking and serving dinner. She could hear the joint sizzling and spluttering behind the big glass door, and saw that the potatoes were beginning to turn a golden brown.

When Pat came he would pour drinks and sit on a stool and watch and talk to her.

It was ten past eight – why was he late? Hovering in her mind's eye were those five stark-sounding words: *You are going to die.* The trouble was that as every moment passed she became more anxious and more aware of the threat, and less capable of hiding that fact that she was worried for more reasons than his lateness, more even than the 'warning' from Gordon Scott.

'Oh, Pat!' she cried aloud. 'Why don't you come?'

As she spoke she heard a faint ring at the front door bell, the warning he always gave of homecoming. She flew into the big room, heart beating very fast; it was incredible that she still felt like this after over twenty years. She pulled open the door into the passage — and there he was stepping inside, a handsome blond giant who for some incredible reason stayed in love with her. He looked bronzed and well, and he carried one large suitcase and a box which was gift-wrapped with green ribbon.

He looked up and saw her.

'Darling!' he cried, and dropped the case as she ran towards him.

He had the most powerful arms and the hug of a bear and yet there was such gentleness in him. He held her very close and she hugged him very tightly, as the self-closing door snapped to behind him.

She held on a shade too long and a shade too tightly, and Dawlish thought: She's scared. It's about those damned Press reports.

He held her a little too firmly, kissed her fractionally harder than she had expected, and she thought: He's worried; it's about the newspapers.

And Dawlish thought, his squeeze tightening: *I must not tell her about the threatening note.*

While Felicity thought, still holding on as if fearful that she would lose him if she let go: Whatever I do I mustn't tell him about the *you are going to die* note.

'Darling ...'

'Sweetheart ...'

'You must be famished.'

'I could eat a Felicity special.'

'This is a Lois special with finishing touches by Felicity.'

'It sounds perfect. Darling ...'

'Sweetheart ... How did it go?'

'On the whole, wonderfully well.'

'Were there many there?'

'Over two hundred – easily a record!'

'That was wonderful. Did you reach any decision?'

'Momentous ones! We are all going to ask our governments for more money!'

'Goody for you!'

'Even Hanlo decided to try hard,' Dawlish enthused.

During this dialogue he had picked up his case, placed the gift packet under his left arm, placed his right arm round Felicity's waist, and walked with her into the main bedroom, with its enormous king-size bed and its huge panoramic window with the lights of London below and the lights of the stars above. He had put the case on a luggage stand and the packet on the bed, then hoisted her clear off the floor so that their faces were level.

He would have been almost too handsome but for a broken nose, the consequences of schoolboy boxing.

31

She was beautiful to him, with her broad features and rather high cheekbones and green-grey eyes and blemishless skin, unless freckles could be considered blemishes. The clusters she had at the base of her nose and on her forehead made her look young again.

'I love you,' he said softly.

'I love you,' she said, huskily.

'Don't stop,' pleaded Dawlish.

'Don't dare to stop,' ordered Felicity.

'No, dear,' promised Dawlish, meekly.

'Darling, I'll go and put dinner out. Shall we eat in the kitchen?'

'Wherever you like. How long may I have?'

'Six minutes.'

'I won't be a second late,' he promised.

He let her down gently, and for a moment they stared at each other but suddenly she turned and hurried away. The door swung to. He stood looking at it, and he thought: It's upset her more than I thought it would. I hope none of those Whitehall wallahs have been worrying her. He crossed to the bathroom, took off his jacket, and washed briskly. There would be plenty of time after dinner to unpack and go through the pile of letters which he saw on Felicity's writing desk. He wished she weren't quite so edgy.

He wished he weren't either. Even to the moment of getting out of the police car which had met him at Heathrow, he had looked about him to make sure he hadn't been followed. But he was already much more himself, and anxious to talk about the conference although he did not want to put any pressure on Felicity.

He was in the big room in precisely six and a half minutes.

Felicity had after all set the dining table for two, the place mats were snow-white against the dark, polished wood, three lighted candles stood up in a three-holder silver candlestick, the cutlery glistened, a bottle of red Burgundy stood on the table near his place. When they dined at home they sat opposite each other, not side by side or at an angle.

He was glad she was making this an occasion.

She came in as he was opening the wine, the beef on a trolley, vegetables on a lower shelf, plates on a hot-plate beneath which a little nightlight glowed. She put out the electric light. He poured the wine and then carved; the knife went easily through the beef, the potatoes had a darker-than-gold lusciousness, the meal was in its way perfect. They talked of people – delegates – and trifles, while Dawlish felt quite sure that Felicity was holding something back. But it would be a long time before the effect of this meal wore off.

Finally, she fetched an apple pie with lashings of whipped cream.

'Marvellous!' he enthused, and demolished a huge helping. He was a man who could eat as much as he liked without putting on weight. He resisted the temptation of a second helping, and Felicity said:

'You sit back, I'll wheel the trolley and bring the coffee.'

'Don't be long,' he said. 'Want any help loading the dishwasher?'

'You sit down and relax,' she ordered.

He lit a small cigar, all he smoked these days, and leaned back in the luxurious comfort of a ten-foot-long settee, and was almost dozing when the telephone bell rang. He lifted the receiver.

'Hallo,' he said.

Felicity lifted the extension in the kitchen, pushing the coffee tray further on to the counter for safety. It was the first time that day she had answered the telephone without a spasm of apprehension.

'Hallo,' she said.

A man answered them in a toneless voice; it was almost as if he were tired out and could hardly find the strength to speak.

'*You are both going to die,*' he declared.

Then the line went dead.

Dawlish was off the couch in a flash, and at the door as Felicity reached it from the other side. She was empty-handed, and very pale as she looked up at him. He pushed the door so that it rode a catch and stayed open, and took her hands. They stood very still for some seconds before he asked:

33

'Is that what was worrying you?'

She nodded.

'So he's called before?'

With an effort she answered: 'This morning. And – I had a letter.'

'Oh,' Dawlish said, face and body relaxing, until he was almost smiling. 'On thick white paper, five words on an old typewriter and folded over and over before it went into the envelope?'

The expression in her eyes flared up.

'You had one, too?'

'Yes,' Dawlish answered, and took out an envelope covered in thin plastic, which had been handed to him just before he had left Zurich. 'Like this?'

'Exactly!' Felicity freed herself and flew to the escritoire, pulled it open and rummaged beneath some papers in the middle drawer. She drew out an envelope, holding it gingerly by one coner; it was white and identical with Dawlish's in colour and shape, the only difference was in the address and the stamp.

'Oh, my sweet!' Dawlish exclaimed. 'Scared stiff?'

'Terrified. I know it's silly, but . . .'

'It's not silly at all. At least, I don't feel silly.'

'And *you're* scared?' She spoke as if that was hard to believe.

'Edgy, yes. I can tell you one thing.'

'What?'

'There were fingerprints on mine. Hanlo is to send a set to me at the Yard. I had the strangest idea that I shouldn't allow the little woman to know about it!'

They both laughed.

'I feel much better,' Felicity declared. 'Much.'

'I think I do, too. Are we going to have any coffee?'

'Oh, what a fool I am, I left it on the bar!'

Felicity swung round and rushed into the kitchen while Dawlish turned away and stared over the skyline of London. There was St. Paul's, under floodlights, several other churches, too, as well as the Tower. The lights from the bridges, from the Embankment and from the great buildings on the South Bank reflected in the smooth surface of the river, making a pattern which was moving all the time but never seemed to change.

His face was set: his expression bleak.

He turned as he heard a chink of cups, and moved a book from a low table so that she could set the coffee tray down. Two deep armchairs were placed here so that while sitting and drinking coffee they could look out over London, but from this spot they had to crane their necks to see the Houses of Parliament and Big Ben.

Felicity poured out.

'Have you any idea who it is?' she asked.

'Not yet,' replied Dawlish.

'Should I have told Gordon Scott? Or someone at the office?'

'No,' Dawlish said. 'Sills is away and Gordon's got his hands full. I'll take these along to the London police tomorrow and ask them to get busy on it. This coffee's very good.'

'Good! Pat . . .'

'What else have you been keeping from me?'

'Quite the worst,' Felicity told him.

'I can believe it.' He placed his great hand over her knee and pressed gently. 'Seriously, darling.'

'I hate to say it,' she said, 'but I *am* serious. I think I would have told Gordon about the note if he hadn't first called me, and . . .' She told Dawlish what Gordon Scott had said, almost word for word, while conveying his sense of disquiet. It was a disquiet which passed itself on to Dawlish, too: the greater because of that morning's reception at the conference and the knowledge that all the delegates felt exactly as he did.

When Felicity had finished, he held out his cup for more coffee.

'You've really had quite a day,' he remarked.

'It wasn't one of the most anxiety-free,' Felicity admitted, with a smile which made her radiant. 'But I've had many, many worse!' They sat holding hands for a few minutes, watching the near-mesmeric scene, and gradually one of the changes which come to men, a kind of metamorphosis, came to Dawlish. He became aware of Felicity not simply as Felicity, but as his woman and his wife, and experience had told him that once such a change came about there were only two courses of action, and one of them was to get up and busy himself with chores, or switch on the television in another

35

corner of the room. The other course was to allow his hands to steal up to her bosom and to draw her back against him.

Soon, his lips were brushing her forehead, her cheeks and her lips.

Soon he said: 'Come to bed, my darling.'

It was still early; not yet eleven o'clock.

They lay apart, looking at each other dreamily, from either side of the huge bed. There was still something enticing about the way the sheet draped over her shoulders – or rather, partly over her shoulders. The soft light from the dressing table heightened her attractiveness, increased his handsomeness.

It was very quiet.

He was beginning to think.

'Pat,' she said, 'it's incredible how one can forget everything.'

'Except the one thing that really matters.'

'Does being in love matter as much to you as that?'

'Yes,' he said, simply. 'Just as much.'

'Pat . . .'

He moved towards her and pressed her lips gently with his.

'Don't harass yourself with those problems and mightbe's, darling. Not now. Tomorrow we can cope.'

'Pat,' she said the moment her mouth was free, 'do you ever feel badly that we didn't have children?'

He didn't answer at first because the question took him so much by surprise, but on reflection he realized that it should not have. There was something about these moments or the moods which followed them that made her almost nostalgic for the children they had never had. In the heyday of their love and sex life little had been known about sterility and barrenness, and too many people had still considered childlessness an act of God. Had they been younger or had as much been known then as there was now, he had little doubt they would have tried to fill the gap. The strange thing was that he was more aware of having no children than he had been even five years ago.

He had to decide whether to lie; tell her a half-lie; or to be honest.

So he said: 'Sometimes, darling, yes. But it doesn't last for long. I think . . .' He broke off, and slid his arms round her so that he drew her warm, smooth body close to his.

'What do you think?' she whispered.

'I think it makes me more aware of how much I depend on you,' he declared.

He saw the tears welling up in her eyes.

CHAPTER FIVE

ATMOSPHERE

HE awoke a little after seven o'clock.

He was fully rested and awake on the instant, but he did not stir at once, simply looked at Felicity. She was way off on the other side of the bed, facing him. There were no signs of tears now, and no sign of distress or unhappiness or alarm. Just peace. Her hair was dishevelled, which was hardly surprising, and the handkerchief he had taken from a bedside cabinet for her tears was poking from beneath her pillow. The white sheet covered her up to her chin.

All she had said, last night, was: 'It's all right, darling, it's all right. That's exactly how I feel.'

Soon afterwards, she had dropped off to sleep.

He had eased himself out of bed, put on a dressing-gown, and gone and looked through the family letters which had arrived during his four days in Switzerland, then read the English newspaper accounts of his speech last night. The trouble with an extempore speech was not that one said what one didn't mean but that one had so little time to watch one's phrasing. Apparently he had said it would be a good idea to let criminals fight things out with one another – a good remark with a group of policemen but one that didn't look well in print for politicians or the general public. And three newspapers quoted him as saying:

Instead of complaining about the failure of the police to catch more criminals, our law-makers might be wiser to change the laws which at present give the criminals far more protection than they give the police or the public.

This phrase had gone through his mind time and time again when at last he had gone to bed. He had thought for a while that he was not going to drop off, but at last he did. And now, with his mind as clear as a bell, he thought:

And that is exactly what we want. A change in laws.

He got out of bed and struggled into a dressing-gown which had a sleeve turned inside out, put a kettle on a low gas, had a quick shower and then made tea. While this brewed he fetched the newspapers from the big letter box in the hall, and squatted on a kitchen stool, drank tea and skimmed the newspapers. There was little comment about the police conference, just the simple statement that it had wound up, except in the *Globe*, where a newspaperman who signed himself Edgar Rapp, had a feature page article with huge headlines:

Should We Keep Our Coppers At Home?

Despite some glib optimism from certain of its delegates, the seventeenth International Police Conference broke up in Zurich yesterday on a note of deep gloom.

Many delegates admitted that they doubted whether it would ever become an effective force.

One or two even doubted whether as an organization it will ever meet again.

The reason for all this gloom? Shortage of money.

That really isn't surprising when one realizes that most civilized [*sic!*] countries and big cities spend a fortune fighting crime. Or, as I have heard it put, failing to fight crime.

If the governments and the civic authorities won't spend enough to keep crime off their own doorsteps, how can one expect them to finance a battle against crimes which take place across the English Channel, across the Atlantic, or on the other side of the world? 'Keep one's coppers at home' is a slogan one might hear loud and clear from many sources and many climes in the next few weeks.

And a question will doubtless be asked:

'Are we our brother's jailers?'

Dawlish put this newspaper down slowly, poured himself more tea, and carried it into the kitchen. He shaved, tried the tea and found it lukewarm and tipped it down the hand basin. He went to his dressing-room and dressed, peeped in at Felicity who hadn't stirred; it was still not eight o'clock. He went into the big room and lifted the telephone and dialled the number of Gordon Scott's flat. The ringing sound went on for so long that he thought the younger man must have left early for the office, but just as he was about to put the receiver down Scott answered breathlessly.

'Gordon Scott!'

'When you've got your breath back I'd like to know how things went yesterday,' Dawlish said.

'Mr. Dawlish!' Scott was still gasping.

'No hurry, Gordon.'

'It – it's all right. I'd just started down the stairs when I heard the bell ring.' The younger man had a small flat at the top of one of the old buildings in the Adelphi, a part of London between the Embankment Gardens and the Strand known by few but loved by nearly all who knew it for its eighteenth century houses and its quietness. But few of the four-storey houses there had lifts, and only the hale and hearty could live there in comfort. 'I'm all right, sir, really.'

'After you'd told my wife of the mood of a lot of people, what followed?' asked Dawlish.

Gordon Scott answered: 'I can't say I liked it, sir.'

'The situation worsened, you mean?'

'In a way, yes, although I wouldn't say the situation worsened, I would say the mood did. I've friends over at the new buildings, of course, and one of the younger members of Parliament is an old friend of mine. The general feeling...' Scott broke off, as if in confusion.

'As if I'd gone too far?' Dawlish said for him.

'Yes and no.' Scott seemed determined to temporize. 'Some of the senior officers do think so – or at least they say they do. And I had five calls from the Home Office and four from the Commissioner – good lord, I forgot! You will be in by ten o'clock, won't you?'

'Yes.'

'I told everyone I was sure you would be,' declared Scott in obvious relief. There was a long pause before he went on with undoubted diffidence: 'It isn't really easy to explain what I mean, sir. I can tell you what I *think*.'

'Tell me exactly what you think,' encouraged Dawlish.

Already, he had a fairly clear picture of the situation as it was developing and it gave him no cause for rejoicing. Nor did Scott's hesitation. The younger man had had plenty of time to assess the situation and had probably rehearsed what he was going to say when they met; nevertheless he was far from at ease. At last, and in a clear, less harried voice, he responded:

'I suppose it's rather like this, sir. We have been through a bad patch in crime, a lot of big jobs have been pulled off in England in the past few months and a lot of people, especially at the new building, are browned off about it. They think their hands are tied – not enough staff, modernization is too slow, that kind of thing. And of course everyone including the Home Office blames the police – that's almost ritual.' Gordon Scott was no fool, reflected Dawlish with some satisfaction. 'And one or two of the newspapers are always slamming the police, which means the Yard. So the mood is pretty low.'

'This I knew,' Dawlish said into a pause.

'I don't need telling that you knew it better than I, sir, and *I* know what you said in Zurich was a deliberate attempt on your part to open the eyes of the Home Office and to show that the police can't work miracles. The war against crime really has to be paid for. The politicians never seem to realize that. But then, they never have.'

Dawlish just stopped himself from saying that was exactly what he had intended, so why all the fuss? The Home Office he could understand, but not the police. He did not ask, however, yet Scott's answer might have been an answer to the spoken question.

'The trouble is, the way it came over is that you were asking for more money for the Crime Haters at a time when there isn't enough for needs at home,' Scott went on, his tone becoming almost desperate. 'And of course, you've come in from the outside, so to speak – you aren't one of *them*. So – well, there *is* resentment at the new building, Mr. Dawlish. You're catching it both ways.'

'Oh,' said Dawlish, very heavily and slowly, 'Now I see.'

'It isn't really personal, sir . . .' began Scott hastily.

'Gordon,' Dawlish interrupted, 'if I were in the shoes of the regular C.I.D. men or even the Special Branch I think I should feel exactly as they do. It doesn't make the situation any easier to take or simpler to deal with, but it's completely understandable.'

After a pause, Scott said huskily: 'You're about the only

man who would see it that way, sir. *I* think it's bloody unfair and I hate having to pass on word about it.'

'You're no help to me if you don't tell me just how things are,' Dawlish said. 'That was no more than the truth. Who is expecting me at ten o'clock?'

'The Commissioner, sir.'

'Is he coming to the office?' Dawlish's voice rose high in surprise.

'It wouldn't surprise me, but he didn't say so,' answered Scott. 'Not in so many words.'

'He wouldn't commit himself,' Dawlish remarked reflectively. 'All right. If he calls again confirm I'll be there, and make no appointments in case he needs most of the morning.'

'Very good, sir,' said Gordon Scott.

Dawlish rang off, and peered at the telephone pensively; inwardly he was more troubled than he liked to admit. The Commissioner of the Metropolitan Police was the senior police official in London, and Dawlish was one of several Assistant Commissioners and Deputy Assistant Commissioners who served under him. There was the A.C. of the Criminal Investigation Branch of which his particular charge was a part; he was the Deputy A.C. who looked after crime which had ramifications abroad. There was the A.C. Special Branch, there were the leaders of the Civil and of the Uniformed Branches – and the Commissioner had to cope with them all.

The present Commissioner was Sir Charles Frazer, fairly recently appointed from the Home Office, a good human being and a first-class administrator, whom Dawlish liked. Frazer would not readily "send" for him because the rumour that he was on the carpet would spread. He would be much more likely to visit Dawlish in his own office for an important discussion. He might even suggest lunch!

Thinking of lunch, he hadn't had breakfast; no wonder he was getting hungry! He sprang to his feet and strode to the kitchen door which opened as he stretched out his hand for it. There stood Felicity, a dressing-gown tied loosely about her, tousled and sleepy-eyed.

'Pat!' she exclaimed. 'I thought you'd gone.'

'Without saying good-morning? Never! Sleep well?'

'Perfectly.'

'All I need now is a little breakfast . . .'

Just after nine o'clock, fortified by bacon and eggs, toast and marmalade and coffee, he went off, while Felicity went back to dress. He missed the sparse-bearded, thin-faced postman who was coming up in one lift while he went down in the other, but Lois Kenning was hurrying into the huge foyer as he went out, trim in an orangey-brown knitted suit.

'Good morning!' he boomed.

Her face lit up.

'Oh, you're back!'

'All safe from furrin parts,' he declared smiling. 'You look very attractive this morning.'

'Thank you, sir!' Lois bobbed a mock curtsy, and went one way as he went the other.

The moment she was out of sight she was out of mind, and he turned right along the Embankment and then right again. He had fallen in love with the penthouse, never dreaming that the day would come when he would find himself within walking distance not only of the "old" New Scotland Yard, on the top floor of which he had his office, but also the "new" New Scotland Yard. By taking side streets and two alleys he came to Victoria Street in ten minutes; and immediately across the road was the towering new building which housed much of the Metropolitan Police.

He knew exactly what to do.

As he reached the opposite pavement two chief superintendents, big men and able men who had reached the top of the C.I.D. tree, came from the direction of Victoria Station, from which they had doubtless walked. In earnest conversation, they did not notice him until he held the doors open for them and said:

'Good morning, gentlemen.'

They looked up – and one was astounded and the other missed a step.

'Er – good morning.'

'Good morning, sir.'

'And a lovely one,' said Dawlish heartily, following them in. He walked alongside them without showing any indication that he knew they were startled. 'I'm back from Zurich with a problem on which I need help from you chaps. You wouldn't know of a superintendent with next-to-nothing to do at the moment, would you?'

The bigger man gulped.

'That will be the day,' said the other, who was taller and leaner.

'Help with what?' inquired the first man.

Before Dawlish could answer they had reached the lifts, and more C.I.D. men appeared from the other main entrance on Broadway. The startled expressions on their faces told Dawlish how right Gordon Scott had been: yesterday his name must have been taken very much in vain in this building. It was a long time since he had been aware of such an atmosphere, less one of hostility than of distrust or wariness. In the days now long ago when he had often carried out investigations independent of – and frequently against the orders of – the police, such an atmosphere had been commonplace. But it was now nearly ten years since he had been an official member of the C.I.D. and superior in rank to all of these men.

Seven men crowded into a lift car.

'Does anyone know where I'll find Commander Liddell?' Dawlish asked at large.

'Probably in the canteen,' one of the younger men volunteered.

'Cafeteria,' another corrected.

'He usually gets in early and does a stint before breakfast,' added a third.

'Thanks,' Dawlish said. 'I'll try there.'

He got out at the 5th floor with several others and walked along to the cafeteria. Almost opposite the main entrance were tables where senior officers usually sat, and there was Liddell, a very heavy-looking, thick-set man with a little dark hair brushed in streaks over his cranium. He was with one of the younger superintendents, and made no attempt to get up as Dawlish approached.

That wasn't simply rude; it was defiance.

CHAPTER SIX

ANGER

THAT was the moment when Dawlish felt a surge of anger.

It was easy to talk as he had to Gordon Scott; to say that in the shoes of these men he would probably feel much the same as they did; it was not easy to accept it and to behave as if everything were normal. He had come to test the mood, and had no doubt that it was wary and even hostile, but this was the first open antagonism he had met. Liddell would normally have got up, or at least made to rise from his chair; and he would have said 'Good morning.' Instead he sat still as a mountain, staring up at Dawlish.

He had muddy brown eyes in his heavy-featured, florid face.

By his side, open at the features page, was a copy of the *Daily Globe*. So he had been reading the article *Should We Keep Our Coppers At Home?* If he looked about him, Dawlish suspected, he would see a dozen copies of the *Globe*, and those who hadn't already seen the article would read it before long.

Dawlish's anger cooled.

It must have shown in his eyes, in the way his jaws were clamped, but it did not express itself in words. Everyone watching knew what was happening, of course, and there were at least fifty C.I.D. men here, from detective officers to chief superintendents. Dawlish was in a rare quandary. He could exert his authority and so make Liddell respond: but if he did he would lose more respect and as far as he could judge he hadn't much left to lose. There was no doubt about the hostility and he could not understand it. For the moment, understanding was less important than dealing with an utterly unexpected situation. What a contrast from last night, at Zurich!

Or he could in effect submit to Liddell's manner: pretend that he had not noticed the form of defiance, pull up a chair and start to talk. This way he would lose at least as much respect and, far worse, he would have allowed Liddell to assume the ascendancy. No assistant commissioner could afford that, any more than a general in the army could allow a colonel to assume even moral control.

The confrontation hadn't lasted long. Another few seconds and it would be an issue. He had virtually decided what to do: say, bluntly, that as he wasn't in the C.I.D. proper he did not want to have to exert pressure, and then stop, with the ball in the other's court. It wasn't wholly satisfactory but would have to serve. Before he began to speak, however, but schooled himself to smile and speak without heat, a man called out from behind him. He recognized the voice on the instant.

'Patrick Dawlish! The very man I want to see!'

Dawlish turned his head and Liddell looked towards the speaker, who was the assistant secretary at the Yard, with no rank and no authority over any of the uniformed or C.I.D. force but a man nevertheless of considerable influence. Whether he had just come in or whether, sensing the situation, he moved from a nearby table, Dawlish did not know. He was short and rather tubby, with glossy silver hair, immaculately dressed; his face was that of a man who sat perpetually in the sun.

He shook hands warmly, as Dawlish said:

'Hallo, Dally. I haven't seen you for ages. How can I help you?'

'It's certainly a long time,' agreed the other whose name was Dalyrymple. 'It really isn't very much, but since Childs retired I never know whether to worry you about such things as overtime sheets or see Sims, who isn't the all-rounder that Childs was. Can I slip over and see you? Or while you're in the building can you come to my office?'

'I've a job to discuss with the commander here,' Dawlish answered, 'and if that doesn't take too long, I'll certainly come down.'

'Tell you what,' said Dalyrymple, 'I'll get myself another cup of coffee.'

He went off, and Dawlish turned to find Liddell on his feet, and the man who had been with him approaching the table bearing two cups of tea or coffee. Liddell had thought better of whatever had been on his mind, and had sent for a kind of olive branch. He had a slight lisp, unexpected in so bull-like a man.

'Like to talk here or in my office?' he asked. The last word sounded like 'offith'.

'Here will do fine,' said Dawlish as they sat down.

'Thought you'd like a cup of coffee, sir.' The man who had been with Liddell placed two cups carefully on the table, and went on hastily to Liddell: 'I'll get on with that job right away, Commander.'

Liddell nodded.

Most eyes were now turned away but a few men still looked towards the pair who were so different in appearance. Dawlish sugared his coffee and stirred with his right hand while he took the two envelopes from his inside breast pocket and handed them to the other man, saying: 'These speak for themselves.' Liddell compared the envelopes, his gaze moving to the stamps, then saw the grey powder marks made when the Swiss police had tested the one for prints.

He looked up. 'Any results?'

'These were done in Switzerland last night, and photo-copies of the prints are on the way. I haven't tested the one addressed to my wife – I didn't know she'd had one until late last night.'

He was half-prepared for Liddell to say: 'You took your time.' But the man made no comment as he took out the folded letter from Dawlish's envelope. He had thick fingers, the tips flat, but well-shaped nails; and he handled the paper as if it were gossamer. He read the five words, then repeated the process with the other envelope; for the first time, he glanced up.

'The one to you was posted the day before the one to your wife but about the same time. It caught the same collection – the postmark on both shows 7.15 p.m.'

Dawlish nodded.

'Anything else?'

'Two telephone calls saying the same thing,' Dawlish answered, and explained in some detail.

'Nasty business,' remarked Liddell, with a frown. 'Something too cryptic to be a joke. You take them seriously, sir, don't you?'

'Very.' That 'sir' was the first overt sign of a change of thinking.

'I'll put Archer on to this right away,' Liddell promised, and Dawlish instantly recalled the name of the man who had been with the commander and had brought his coffee. 'If you get anything else you'll let me know, won't you?'

'At once,' Dawlish promised.

'Thanks. Sorry it's happened,' Liddell told him, and repeated: 'Nasty. I never like it when they start worrying the family. Will you be in London for a while, sir?'

Now the relationship between them was wholly normal.

Dawlish smiled. 'I'll even be in my office most of the time unless I get thrown out for my recent indiscretions!' He got up, glad to see those muddy eyes and set lips take on a hint of a smile. 'Thanks, Commander. Now I'd better go and see how much of the taxpayer's money we've been spending on overtime!' He went across to Dalyrymple, who stood up immediately, and they walked together. 'Dally,' Dawlish said as they neared the door, 'I can't spare more than a few minutes.'

'That's all we need,' Dalyrymple assured him. 'And we could do that over the telephone! I wanted to get our stubborn commander off the hook he'd fashioned for himself!'

'I wondered if that was what you were up to,' Dawlish said appreciatively. 'For the time being we're both off the hook, it seems.'

Dalyrymple turned into the door of his office, a square one with windows overlooking the courtyard of the new building, closed the door firmly and went to his desk. In the next room, approached by a communicating door, was his secretary and two assistants. He turned to face Dawlish very steadily.

'Pat,' he said, 'I mustn't take sides and I won't even attempt to. But I'm not the only one here who is quietly rooting for you.'

'Ah,' said Dawlish. 'Thank you. Can you answer me one question?'

'I hope so.'

'How many of the top brass wallahs are after my blood?'

Dalyrymple pursed lips then shook his head slowly and answered:

'I don't know. I don't really understand what's happened. I think it's simply a matter of frayed nerves, and quite suddenly you found yourself blamed not for causing the situation but for making the inflammation worse. Everyone here knows we coppers need more money, that's nothing new, and . . .' He gave a strangled laugh. 'I suppose the truth is that a lot of them are afraid you might get some for your Crime Haters and leave the regulars out in the cold.'

'By pulling strings?' hazarded Dawlish. 'Old school tie, that kind of thing?'

'Yes, that's it,' Dalrymple answered. 'Undue influence of some kind, anyhow. And they don't want you to get it. If any more money is going to the police they want it spent here in England. Could even go further,' Dalrymple went on with a droll grin. 'They want it spent here in London, in fact, certainly not in outlandish parts of the world – especially Switzerland.'

'Eh?'

'Land of the gnomes who have all of our money,' explained Dalrymple. 'If you want it in the plainest language, the question is this: when we have to think twice about paying a few men a few pounds overtime, why should we in effect subsidize countries like Switzerland, West Germany, Japan, the United States and so . . .'

'*Ad infinitum*,' Dawlish finished for him. After a long pause, with his lips pursed, he exuded a long, slow breath, and then said bitterly: 'The blind, blind fools.'

'Possibly,' said Dalrymple. 'But don't say it aloud.'

'I won't,' Dawlish promised. 'And thanks. *Warm* thanks, Dally.'

He shook hands and walked out; and he was in the foyer before he realized that he had no idea whether Dalrymple had really wanted to talk to him about chits for overtime which had been put through his department.

It was nearly five to ten.

He could not possibly walk to the old building in five minutes, and might need ten or fifteen even by taxi. As the thought entered his head a taxi approached, its '*For Hire*' sign alight, and he waved it down. Victoria Street and Parliament Square were almost empty of traffic, and he was at the lift leading from the old Flying Squad courtyard at ten o'clock precisely. Two minutes later when he opened the door of his office, an anxious Scott's voice was raised in what was positively a paean of delighted relief.

49

'Here he is, sir!' He clutched the telephone to his bosom and whispered: 'It's the Commissioner, sir!'

'Thanks.' Dawlish took the telephone, rounded his desk and sat down in a large, leather-covered armchair of contemporary design, leaned back and wiped his forehead with his free hand as he said: 'Dawlish here, sir. I'm sorry if I kept you.'

'I am coming straight over to see you,' announced Sir Charles Frazer in his clipped and over-precise voice. 'Sir Arbuthnot Lane will be joining us at eleven-fifteen. Will you arrange not to be disturbed from the time I get there until twelve-thirty?'

'Gladly,' Dawlish answered as crisply.

'Thank you,' said the Commissioner, and he rang off without another word.

Dawlish passed his hand through his wavy hair, the colour of corn, and sat back. He had at most twenty minutes to get ready for the Commissioner, and probably his best bet was to go through reports on cases which had been pending when he had left for Switzerland, and get a verbal report on the Swiss Conference ready to present.

Aloud, he growled: 'I know that inside out.' He sat upright and rigid in his chair, as the glimmering of a new idea flashed into his mind. It was on the perimeter of his thoughts like something which had been hovering but hadn't settled in any one place yet.

Being *here* helped.

Being within hand's reach of a telephone which would let him speak to any police force in the world . . .

He looked about the office, which had smaller windows with views not unlike those from the penthouse, then stretched out a hand and pressed the bell for Gordon Scott. The glimmering was taking shape, with the right help he could prepare the picture clearly before Frazer came. He pulled the sheaf of reports close to him, and called out as the door opened:

'Gordon, I want a summary of every crime committed in this country in the past year where the proceeds are (a) known or (b) believed to have been sent abroad. Get on it yourself and get everyone else cracking. It needn't be absolutely accurate but must be reasonably near.'

As he gave the instructions another thought scintillated

off the perimeter of his mind. Gordon Scott was a first-class man outside the office, a thoroughly reliable policeman and detective but he wasn't the kind of right-hand man he, Dawlish, needed here. Until a year ago there had been exactly the right officer in Jim Childs, who had now retired and who would have this kind of information at his fingertips. Recently a man named Sims had shown promise, but was too often away on sick leave; there was an ugly suspicion of cancer. Childs had also been succeeded by yet another man good for outside work, but not for the records, not really for this kind of job. Well, he had to make do with what help he had.

Childs said from behind him in a quiet, laconic voice: 'If we covered the past six months it would be easier and just as impressive.'

Dawlish spun round in the easy chair.

'Good lord!' he exclaimed. 'A ghost?'

'I looked in because I thought I might be useful,' declared Childs.

Dawlish got up, hand outstretched.

'I've never been so glad to see anybody!'

'I hope you won't be so glad to see the back of me,' Childs said, but obviously he was pleased by such warmth of reception. 'I take it you need to make a quick impression on some VIPs with this information.'

He looked younger than when he had retired; not at all haggard, in fact tanned and calm-eyed. His handgrip was very firm.

'The quickest impression,' Dawlish agreed. 'The Commissioner and the Permanent Secretary of the Home Office are coming, the Commissioner probably first. I want to be able to show them both some figures to prove that what we're doing is an extension of the job being done in London. I can do the talking but I need the figures to sound convincing.'

'I see exactly what you mean,' said Childs, already on the move.

'Where's Scott?' asked Dawlish.

'There was a call from Brussels. The Belgian police think a jewel thief named Griell came over to Heathrow this morning with fifty thousand pounds' worth of stolen jewels. Scott thinks he knows where Griell might be going to sell the loot.

51

Dawlish gave a fierce grin.

'Pray that he finds out for sure! Oh – and keep every call away from me once my visitors come except anything you think is vitally urgent.'

'I'll do that,' promised Childs. 'Shall I show the Commissioner straight in as soon as he comes?'

'The very moment,' Dawlish urged. Childs nodded understanding and went out. The door had hardly closed on him before Dawlish's direct-to-exchange telephone bell rang; and he picked it up with a movement so swift it had a note of savagery in it.

'Dawlish,' he said brusquely.

'I am quite serious,' said a man with a lifeless voice. 'You are going to die – and soon. So is your wife.'

CHAPTER SEVEN

DAWLISH LAUGHS

DAWLISH caught his breath.

At any other time, when he had not been so preoccupied with fighting back on the other issue, he might have been badly shaken. As it was, he was at first startled, then angry, and suddenly, gloriously aggressive. The other man's receiver had not yet gone down, he was sure he could hear soft breathing.

'Not on your life,' he said. 'I'll break your neck long before you can cause us any harm. Get off the line, I'm busy.'

More sharply, the man said: 'Dawlish, you'll regret this!'

Dawlish actually laughed. It was not derisive laughter and it wasn't hearty, rather an amused chuckle, followed by a brusque: 'You'd be surprised how often I've been told that.'

He rang off.

He sat still for a moment, and then ran the back of his hand across his forehead; he was surprised how much sweat was on it. He dialled the new Scotland Yard, and asked for Chief Inspector Archer; Archer came on almost at once.

'Dawlish,' Dawlish said.

'I'm having your wife watched, sir,' Archer stated promptly. 'And you whenever it's practicable.'

'Thanks,' Dawlish said gruffly. 'The chap has just had another go at me on the telephone. Too many people know it, by the way, I've had it too long – get a different number, will you?' As Archer promised to do so, he went on: 'The only thing he added was that we were to die "soon". I'm not sure that I handled it well, but . . .'

'Exactly how did you handle it?' Archer asked.

Dawlish hesitated.

There were detectives and detectives. The first kind were those who worked with a rough knowledge of the facts and moved by a mixture of hunch and instinct. He was one of these and there were a surprising number of others who used the method even at the Yard. The second kind of detective was comprised of those who needed and used every tiny detail; who solved a problem much as one fitted in all the pieces of a jig-saw puzzle. He did not know Archer well but began to suspect that he was one of the second kind.

'If I tell you precisely can you take it down so that I don't have to repeat?' he asked. 'I've a conference...'

'I shall remember,' Archer stated matter-of-factly.

'Oh,' ejaculated Dawlish, and his lips worked in a rueful smile. 'Good. Ready?'

'Quite ready, sir.'

Dawlish told him exactly what had happened, the precise time of the call, his own responses and even his own succession of moods, and Archer did not interrupt with comment or question. Almost as soon as Dawlish had finished, however, the chief inspector asked:

'Have you the slightest idea who this might be, sir?'

'None,' answered Dawlish.

'Will you give the possible identity as much concentrated thought as you can and as soon as you can?'

'Yes.'

'Thank you. Have you told your own staff about this?'

'Not yet,' answered Dawlish.

'Will you, sir, please? They may have more idea of who may be uttering these threats than you – may be more aware of anyone who thinks he has special cause to hate you and your wife – or you or your wife,' Archer amended. 'The more details I can get and the more possible indications the better. One other thing, sir.'

'What thing?' asked Dawlish, looking at an electric clock in one of the big desks in the room. The dial was shaded and marked in such a way that it showed the hour in every time zone and so every country in the world.

'May I go and see your wife?'

The Commissioner would be here any minute now.

'Yes,' Dawlish answered, 'but telephone her first, please.'

'Be sure I'll do that,' Archer assured him. 'Thank you, sir. I'll report as soon as I've anything useful to say.'

Dawlish and the other man rang off simultaneously, but

the call had slowed down Dawlish's reactions and responses. He sat with his hand on the telephone, still acutely aware of Archer's voice: a Londoner's voice, not Cockney but with Cockney overtones in the nasal vowel sounds and the briskness. One thing had emerged: both Liddell and Archer were taking the letters in great earnest, which should set his mind at rest for other problems.

Why had the two problems come at once? Was that sheer coincidence?

He took his hand off the one telephone as another, the inter-office one, buzzed; he lifted it, expecting from Childs exactly what he said:

'The Commissioner's just stepping out of the lift, sir.'

'Thanks,' said Dawlish, and he stood up and moved so that he stood with his back to the window, facing the door. He had to wait longer than he expected for the door to open, but not long enough for his attention to wander.

It opened at last and Childs stood on one side, announcing: 'The Commissioner, sir.'

'Ah, Sir Charles!' Dawlish infused warmth into his voice and moved towards Frazer. 'How are you?' The door closed and these two men, leaders in their field, were alone. They shook hands, each with a firm grip, Dawlish a shade taller, more than a shade bigger. But standing by himself, Sir Charles Frazer would have seemed a very large man indeed.

He startled one at first meeting, because he was as bald as Yul Brynner.

The curious thing was that he had well-marked eyebrows, nearly white, and a white moustache obviously well groomed – not waxed but looking as if it had been. His features were very regular, his face thin; he was an impassive-looking man; and somehow impressive, too.

He moved towards the window.

'I think I should exchange offices,' he remarked. 'I look out on an unending expanse of roofs.' He paused to reflect only for a moment, and then turned to glance about the room. Without comment, he went on: 'Dawlish, I am neither with you nor for you. Since I've been at the Yard I've been so deeply preoccupied that I've let well alone where I felt I could, and I certainly felt I could with you. I didn't give you enough thought or attention, it might have helped to head

55

this thing off had I done so. Coming here, for instance, I realized that I've never been to your office before.'

'No,' Dawlish agreed, and said heavily: 'So you're neither with me nor for me.'

'Because I really don't have the facts. Can you brief me in half an hour?' He smiled, faintly; it was in character that he should twirl his moustache briefly. His eyes were hazel brown, as clear as Liddell's were muddy.

'Yes,' answered Dawlish. 'But what is there to be for or against me about? What is the issue?'

'You mean you don't know?'

'I've heard some rumours and I can cut the atmosphere at the new building with a knife. But at most I made an indiscreet speech in Zurich. I'm not even sure it was indiscreet,' he added wryly. 'I think had I known what kind of furore it was going to create I would have pitched it higher and stronger.'

'Oh,' said Frazer. 'So you do.' His smile had gone, he was wholly serious. 'Didn't you get my letter in Zurich?'

'No,' answered Dawlish.

Frazer was taken aback enough to say: *'Why the hell didn't it reach you?'* in an aside uttered with such feeling that Dawlish felt a new wave of apprehension. They stood facing each other, and Dawlish's apprehension increased, for the issue was obviously much more significant than he had realized. They did not move. Their backs were to the windows and they faced the office which was also a highly sophisticated communications centre, installed during Dawlish's early months here. The equipment in this room was, next to salaries, by far the most serious expense item on the department's budget.

Sir Charles Frazer took no notice of the office itself but studied Dawlish and gave the impression that he was trying to find the right words; trying not to be too upsetting.

At last, he said: 'The Home Secretary wants to disband your department, and incorporate parts of it in the new building. He has had a committee working on this for several months. I had put in a request for a thirty per cent higher budget for the Metropolitan Police Force as a whole, and the official response – although I didn't hear about this until Friday – was that there must be severe economies in some fields if there is to be more money available in others.'

His voice stopped: the silence which followed reflected Dawlish's shock.

For a few seconds he could not even think clearly, only one sentence burned itself into his mind, a sentence so unbelievable he could not really believe it had been uttered. *'The Home Secretary wants to disband your department.'* Slowly, he began to feel anger seeping into his veins; became aware that the colour had faded from his cheeks, his lips had tightened, his eyes narrowed until all Frazer could see were slits of vivid blue. And he began to breathe heavily but through his nostrils, making his chest rise and fall.

Frazer did not look away from him.

A sound other than his own breathing seemed to fall upon his ears and then fill his head. Applause. The clapping and the stamping of two hundred policemen from all over the world. A sight other than Frazer's face and head and shoulders appeared before his eyes – his mind's eyes. The delegates in Zurich rising to their feet, while the applause became a roar and interspersed were cheers and the sound of his name.

'Dawlish – Dawlish – Dawlish!'

Suddenly, he moved his right arm, gripped Frazer's shoulder, and urged him towards the centre of the room. He began to speak in a low-pitched, angry voice, but the anger he showed was so much less than the rage he felt.

He pointed at a panel which stretched half-way across the room, a projection of the world, showing every country in different pastel colours, with a small circle showing each major city and dots showing countless others. The whole world was stretched out in front of him, and along the panel were switches and telephones. He pressed a switch and a dozen lights showed at circles, twice as many pinpricks of lights at the dots. Above the telephone a word glowed: *Hold.*

'See that?' he growled. 'I can get in touch with any one of the world's police forces in a second – national and metropolitan police forces *everywhere* in the world. I can send to each of them an identical request for information or statement of information and have a response back here in minutes – whether from Tokyo or Moscow, Montreal or Buenos Aires. I can send a description of stolen goods and of wanted men out as quickly as I can flick that switch. I've five

57

men in the next room, monitoring this information panel – it makes the one in the new building look like a child's toy.

'And *look!*' He spun Frazer round to a second panel which joined the other at right angles. Across the right angle itself was his desk, with its telephones and its drawers, its files, everything he needed. He pointed at the second panel as he spoke, his voice rising but still completely under control. This was another projection of the world, with cities marked in large areas, colours and shading of every possible variation, and a criss-cross of lines over lands and over oceans. He pressed button after button and the lines lit up. He tapped the dozens which crossed the Atlantic Ocean, and went on: 'Every solid line an air route, every broken line a sea route or on land a railway, every line of dots a trunk road. Every crossed swords a custom office – and every office can get in touch with the nearest police who can get in touch with this office in *minutes.*'

He stopped abruptly, as a low-pitched buzz sounded.

He switched off, but a light glowed at a spot on the border between France and Spain, near the Costa Brava. A man spoke in Spanish but an English translation followed almost at once.

'*Suspect Formazzia detained and car searched diamonds and emeralds found in spare tyre suspect being held until identification of jewels positive.*'

The light went out, and Dawlish picked up a telephone. A man's voice came clearly over a loudspeaker.

'Yes, sir.'

'When did we send the message about Formazzia?'

'Forty-eight hours ago, sir. He was known to have crossed the Channel and believed to have rented a car.'

'Right. Thanks,' Dawlish said. He put the receiver on its hook, and at last released Frazer's shoulder. Frazer showed no sign of discomfort, not even wriggling his arm. Dawlish pushed a chair forward and when Frazer was sitting, dropped into his own. His forehead was wet with sweat but his colour was better and his voice less tense. 'I simply don't understand it,' he said. 'Six months ago, largely through this department, we broke up the English end of the Farenza, an organization which was corrupting industry and commerce all over the country, as well as much of the world. To talk of disbanding is sheer idiocy.'

'No one has said the department doesn't do a good job,' replied Frazer. 'The committee report simply says it could be done more cheaply if it were housed at the new building and were part of the normal work of the Criminal Investigation Department.'

'Well,' grunted Dawlish, 'it couldn't.'

Another fact grew into his mind, now. If Liddell and some of the other C.I.D. men knew about this, then they would think his speech in Zurich was, directly or indirectly, a reflection on them. That would explain their attitude.

'As I told you, I'm neither for nor against you,' Frazer repeated. 'All I know is that we need ten million pounds a year more for police work in England and Wales, and the committee estimates that three million could be saved by moving this office and relying on the normal commercial means of communication instead of maintaining yours. The contribution made last year to the International Police Conference was a hundred thousand pounds apart from the expense here, and that in itself would be a substantial saving. This has grown into a department of its own – the committee says it has grown too big. And some of the regular C.I.D. officers stated to the committee that there is a great deal of overlapping, a great deal of wastage in staff as well as in office space. These factors have to be taken into account.'

So the C.I.D. probably did know what was in the wind.

Dawlish said, in a stiff voice: 'Do you mean this committee took statements from the other departments but not from here?'

'They would hardly expect you or your staff to be objective, would they?' asked Frazer. 'The cost of this section of the department is known. The questions are whether that cost can be substantially reduced without seriously impairing efficiency by transferring the work to the new building. And Dawlish – Sir Arbuthnot Lane will be here very soon, and won't be at all impressed by a demonstration of emotion or histrionics. And I really must say – nor am I.'

CHAPTER EIGHT

MOMENT OF TRUTH

THAT was the moment when Dawlish realized that Frazer did not mean that he was on neither side; the moment when Dawlish understood that the other man was virtually committed, possibly because he was a direct servant of the Home Office; and it was the moment when Dawlish fully understood how long the campaign had been going on. His bluntness at Zurich had simply been the signal for action.

It was an ugly moment.

He knew on the instant what he must do, but sheered away, not wanting even to think about it.

He did not speak at once, but turned to the operations panel and crossed to two small couches placed in the window bay. Frazer followed him. Dawlish stood looking over the river and the skyline, so familiar and so beloved. It was twenty to twelve, so Lane would be here in a few minutes. He, Dawlish, had simply to stall until then. He picked up a telephone from the table between the couches, and it was both good and painful to hear Childs' voice in response.

'Yes, sir.'

'Have coffee and biscuits sent in as soon as Sir Arbuthnot arrives,' he ordered. 'And bring him in at once, please.'

'I'll see to it.'

'Is Scott back?' asked Dawlish.

'No, but Sills telephoned,' said Childs. Sills was one of the men who had replaced him on his retirement. 'He would like to come and see you this afternoon.'

'Did he tell you what it was about?' asked Dawlish.

He was talking partly for the sake of talking, acutely aware of Frazer alternately looking at him and out of the window, and he did not want to speak again to the Commissioner until Lane was here. So although he heard he did not at first fully understand what Childs was saying.

'I think I know what it's about, sir, and in one way he's not happy about it. In another . . .'

Dawlish understood that fully; and he also knew Childs was worried or he would not have persisted so.

'What is it about, then?'

'I think Sir Arbuthnot . . .'

'What *is* it about, Childs?' Dawlish demanded sharply.

'Well,' replied Childs resignedly, 'Sills has been offered the job of Chief Constable of one of the new Federation Groups, and he can't really turn it down. He doesn't like leaving here, especially leaving you, but . . . here *is* Sir Arbuthnot, sir!'

Dawlish said slowly: 'Show him in.'

He replaced the receiver very slowly, and looked at Frazer, who averted his gaze noticeably. There was only seconds between that moment and the moment when the door opened, but it was long enough for Dawlish to understand the full significance of what had happened with his new second-in-command. Sills had been bribed away. Of course he couldn't afford to refuse such a job; few professional policemen could. The old county police forces were being merged, two or three counties into an integral police federation, and few denied that it was a great step forward in efficiency and it even meant some saving of money. But to offer the job as Chief Constable at one of these federations to his, Dawlish's, closest associate without consulting Dawlish was arbitrary; unforgivable.

The door opened, and Childs announced: 'Sir Arbuthnot Lane, sir.'

Lane was a very different man from either Dawlish or Frazer. He was as tall as Frazer, very thin, sharp-featured, pale-faced, with such a crop of wavy nut-brown hair that one sprang immediately to the conclusion that it was either a wig or dyed and artificially waved. He had a heart-shaped mouth and a pointed chin. This morning he wore a suit of medium grey, not the formal black jacket and striped trousers.

He proffered his hand.

Dawlish hesitated for a split second before taking it, then decided that no matter what he thought he must observe the normal courtesies. Lane had an over-hearty handshake or else was being over-hearty for the occasion. He moved across to Frazer, as the door opened and a middle-aged woman with nice legs brought in coffee and biscuits. Momentarily, Dawlish was reminded of Lois Kenning. Then he poured out coffee with the usual questions: 'Black? Milk? Cream? Sugar?' and they settled down, Frazer and Lane on one couch, opposite Dawlish.

Dawlish had himself under complete control now, and asked:

'Well – who's in the chair?'

'Oh, we needn't be formal, not formal at all,' Lane assured him. 'This is just an exchange of views – eh, Commissioner? So that we can have a clear – the clearest – understanding.'

'We certainly need that,' murmured Dawlish.

'I am glad we are in agreement so far!' Lane was almost playful. 'Dawlish, we face – the Government faces, this nation faces – a period of grave economic crisis and so there is a call for the greatest stringency. We at the Home Office, like all other government departments I may say, are constantly looking for ways in which to economize. I will make no bones about it: your department, or rather your section of the Criminal Investigation Department, offers scope for very substantial economies. The Commissioner here has presented us with a reasonable budget for the work of the police at home – within our national boundaries, that is – and we must try to meet it. We cannot, without making cuts in your – very high, I may say – expenditure.'

His voice went on and on, precise, somewhat didactic; headmasterish. Most of what he said was in political clichés – the economic problems, home tasks must come first, one liked to take the distant view but one had to consider the pressing problems of the moment.

When he stopped, Dawlish simply said: 'I see.'

'And while I am here I am charged with two other tasks,' said Lane, severely. 'It has become increasingly your custom to take action, to commit the Home Office and British police forces to activities and expenditure which have not been approved in advance. That simply is not advisable. I am sure that upon reflection you will see that. It will be necessary in future to consult with the Commissioner on major journeys whether of an investigatory or an administrative nature. The Commissioner will undoubtedly have a clear picture of the overall situation – whether your services would be of greater value in London, for instance, than in say' – Lane raised his head challengingly – 'Switzerland. Or Nice in the South of France. Or San Francisco. All of these are among the places where conferences have been held.'

He paused, but still Dawlish said nothing.

'The other task,' went on Lane, 'is to remind you that no public servant is justified in or permitted to make speeches which do not accord with official policy. Your address to the International Police Conference on the night before last was, in fact, in direct contradiction of that policy as well as the policy of cutting down on expenses in the section which you represent.' Again Lane's head went up in that challenging way. 'You do understand why this is necessary, don't you?'

Dawlish actually forced a smile.

'Whether I understand or not seems irrelevant,' he said, standing up. 'More coffee?' He poured out for both of them and added: 'I won't be a moment.' He went to his desk where he was hidden from them, so that they could not see his expression, and for a few moments it was very bleak indeed. He heard them whispering as he took a sheet of his personal notepaper, headed:

Deputy Assistant Commissioner's Office
Criminal Investigation Department
New Scotland Yard, London, SW 1.

He dated the sheet, and wrote:

For the Attention of the Commissioner of the Metro-
politan police
  Sir,
  Please accept this as my formal resignation from your
organization.
            Yours faithfully,

He signed this, folded it and stuffed it into an envelope which in turn he put in his inside breast pocket, and then he went back to the others. As he did so there was a tap at the door and Childs appeared, a paper in his hand.

'What is it?' Dawlish asked.

'Scott just called to say that the Belgian was picked up at Frayer's in Hatton Gardens, with the jewels.'

'Good,' Dawlish said. 'More?'

'Yes. You asked for the details of thefts of goods known to have been sent abroad. Including the theft of old masters valued at three million pounds, and treasury notes of half that amount, the grand total in the past six months is over ten million pounds' worth. Half of this has already been recovered by other national police forces co-operating with us. The summary is here. In addition we have arranged the extradition from other countries of seventeen wanted men, three of whom have since been convicted of murder.' He gave the paper to Dawlish who felt a little better as he rejoined the others, and said almost casually: 'We had a report from Brussels this morning that a thief was supposed to be coming to London. He has been picked up.'

'Could he not have been picked up had the message gone to the new building?' demanded Lane.

'Possibly,' Dawlish admitted. 'If they had all the specialized knowledge, the International Rogues' Gallery and the men to send out the moment there was such a report.'

'Can you explain how this – ah – apprehension helps *us*?' demanded Lane.

Frazer, who had said very little, looked out of the window, as if he realized the crassness of that question.

Dawlish's expression was wooden.

'We have a jewel thief who will be in a Belgian gaol instead of busy burglarizing London,' he said. 'We have strengthened the goodwill between the police of two capital cities. Brussels may pick up a man for us tomorrow.'

'Are you implying that such goodwill did not exist before you were put in charge of your – ah – section?' demanded Lane.

'No,' answered Dawlish, with a smile which became suddenly bright. 'There was a lot of goodwill and even more misunderstanding. Every man on my staff, for instance, can speak several languages, and – but these things you would have discovered if your committee had come here as well as to the new building.'

'Your enthusiasm for your section so obviously outweighs your objectivity,' Lane said severely.

'And your prejudice makes it quite impossible for you to be objective or for me to continue to work under your department,' Dawlish said, and chose this moment to hand his note to Frazer, together with the summary.

Lane actually opened his mouth without uttering a word.

'Dawlish . . .' began Frazer, and then took out the note, read it, and said: 'This is premature. Far too premature.'

'Like offering my chief *aide* a Chief Constable's job?' Dawlish asked evenly. 'You really are the most conniving and knife-in-back pair I have ever met. There is one thing worse than disloyalty from the ranks or junior officers to a commanding officer, and that is disloyalty from a commanding officer to those in his command.' He looked down on them both and went on: 'Quite literally, you make me sick.'

'How dare you talk to the representative of the Home Secretary in such a way?' demanded Lane; he could not prevent his voice from becoming shrill. He saw the notes held out towards him and took them from Frazer, who was now getting to his feet. He read the resignation and then went on in a triumphant way which was really quite sickening to behold. 'But you cannot do this. You are under agreement to give three months' notice.'

'And if I were, you would keep me to it, wouldn't you,' Dawlish said bitingly. 'You're not only blinkered but you are shockingly inefficient.'

'Dawlish!' Lane rose to his feet, one finger pointing at Dawlish.

'If you'd taken the trouble to read my file you'd know that when I signed on the then Home Secretary and the then Commissioner doubted whether they could stand me for a week. And I doubted whether I could stand the red tape and the bumbling I knew was inevitable. So my agreement gives either party the right to resign at a moment's notice. I have resigned.'

Frazer began: 'Now, really, Dawlish, this can't do the C.I.D. or your section of it any good. Be reasonable and . . .'

'I am seeing reason very clearly,' Dawlish said. 'I am now a free citizen not under contract to you, or the Home Office, not under your control or theirs. I am now free to say exactly what I want to say to the Press, within the limits of the Official Secrets Act. I am free to tell the world that the International Police Conference is in desperate need of funds and that you will not increase your allotment and in fact seriously contemplate deserting it. I am free to say I resigned because I don't think this department can work effectively with the economics you propose to force upon it and am not going to try.' He moved towards the door, still facing them. 'If I'm pushed I will also tell the Press that your precious committee didn't trouble to consult me or anyone in the section about your plans, and that Sills was taken away without a by-your-leave. *If* I'm pushed,' he added savagely. 'I hope you won't push me.'

He turned and opened the door.

'Dawlish!' cried Frazer.

'Dawlish . . .' called Lane, and there was an edge which might have been fear in his voice.

'I shall be at my home and available for consultation at any time within reason,' Dawlish said over his shoulder. 'Good day, gentlemen.'

He strode out.

Only Childs was in the room beyond, and he twisted round in his chair, obviously startled. Dawlish, hard-faced and tight-lipped, gripped his shoulder and then went out by the door which led to the hallway and the lifts. A man called out: 'Urgent message for you, sir!' but he ignored it. He did not want to see the others in the department, many of whom he had known for ten years and more. He was not even positive that he had done the right thing, but right or wrong he knew that he could not have continued to work under the domination of those two men.

But a shadow already loomed over him.

He *had* resigned.

This could well be the last time he would enter the office and the department – the 'section', damn their eyes! – which he had created and developed; the materialization of a dream. He had a hazy picture of the delegates at Zurich rising to their feet; he heard as if from a long way off the crash of applause. The picture was shadowed and the sound was very faint. A lift came up, empty, and he went down at once, staring blindly at the sliding doors which had scratches made when this building had been the only home of New Scotland Yard.

He reached the foyer – the old back entrance. No one he knew was there. He half-expected Scott to appear but did not want to see or talk to him yet, he needed to cool off. He went on to the Embankment and strode towards Big Ben and

Parliament Square, still tight-lipped and hard-eyed. Every time he reached a pedestrian crossing the lights turned to *Cross Now* and nothing impeded his passage. Policemen who knew him well by sight stared as if baffled by the way he looked, the way he strode on, his long legs covering the ground at astonishing speed.

He passed the courtyard to the House of Commons, the St. Stephen's entrance to the House of Lords, the gothic magnificence unnoticed as it rose above him. He did not glance right or left but soon reached the approach to Lambeth Bridge and – traffic on the crossings favouring him – strode across to the far side of the Embankment.

He was now within reach of the modern building where he had his home.

It had one main entrance off the Embankment, another at the side, and he chose this way in. Had he chosen the main entrance he would have seen the ambulance waiting and the police outside. As it was, he went in from the side, as the lift doors opened. Two policemen were here where none would normally be, and one held the lift doors while a man in white backed out.

He was an ambulance man.

He was carrying one end of a stretcher.

Dawlish's heart seemed to expand and explode within him as he rushed forward. The second ambulance man held the other, top end of the stretcher, and Dawlish saw Felicity, ashen pale and apparently unconscious, being carried out.

CHAPTER NINE

POISON

WITH the ambulance men was a youngish man who still had a stethoscope round his neck. He glanced at Dawlish without recognition, but one of the policemen said in a gruff voice:

'Sorry about this, Mr. Dawlish.'

The doctor missed a step and looked up; the ambulance bearers went on their slow and steady way. The revolving doors of the main entrance were folded back and the ambulance with other policemen near it was just outside, its doors wide open; gaping.

'Mr. Dawlish?' the doctor asked.

'Yes. How is she?'

'Touch and go,' the young man said.

Touch and go – Felicity? It didn't make sense; it made even less sense than some of the things that had been said to him at his office. He did not really take it in. It was happening and yet he did not seem to be part of it – any more than the *real* he had been involved in the scene at his office.

'We shall do everything we can,' the doctor promised.

'What happened?'

'Poison.'

'What poison?'

'Arsenic.'

'God! Have you used . . .'

'A stomach pump, yes. Mr. Dawlish . . .'

'Where are you taking her?'

'Westminster Hospital,' the doctor answered.

'Is she . . .' He could not bring himself to finish.

'I think she has a chance. I must get her to the hospital at once, I've alerted the ward. If there's a turn either way, I'll let you know immediately.'

Dawlish saw that the stretcher was inside, one of the ambulance men had gone, the other was obviously waiting for the doctor. In a series of vivid flashes facts passed through his mind. Minutes could count. He could not help only hinder. The hospital was only a short distance away. He felt cold sweat break out over his body and face as he went with the doctor, who climbed in nimbly. There was a view, a fore-shortened view, of Felicity's face. The doctor turned towards her, sitting on a lever-seat. The ambulance attendant closed the door and hurried to the front, to join his partner.

Dawlish stood at the revolving doors and watched them drive his wife away. Words hovered like echoes in his mind.

'What happened?'

'Poison.'

'What Poison?'

Arsenic.'

And there was another echoing voice, without tone or emotion of any kind.

'You are going to die ... You are going to die soon ... both of you.'

A policeman asked huskily: 'Are you all right?'

Dawlish stared at him, yet hardly saw him, then went to the lifts, one of which had been kept open. A doorman was by it. 'I'm terribly sorry, sir.' A policeman stepped in after Dawlish and pressed P.H. – the Penthouse button. Dawlish's jaw worked and he felt hot and cold. Neither man spoke, and at last the car reached the top floor.

Dawlish stepped out.

There were two more policemen. There was a young man, who looked little more than a boy, a puny-looking youth with rimless glasses, to whom a policeman was saying:

'Not a chance.'

This youth looked at Dawlish, opened his lips but said nothing. It was reminiscent of Lane a thousand years ago. The front door of the flat was open and Dawlish went in. Two men in plainclothes were in the big room, the door of which was open; and the door from it to the kitchen was standing open on its catch, too. For the first time Dawlish found his voice, demanding: 'Why wasn't I told?'

A policeman answered: 'You'd just left your office, sir.'

A man was saying out of sight: 'I want the truth.'

A woman replied in a tense voice: 'I've told you the truth!'

'Did you bring those chocolates?'

'Yes I did!'

'Did you know some of them had enough poison to kill a dozen human beings?'

'No!' the woman cried.

She was Lois Kenning. When Dawlish reached the communicating door he saw her on one side of the bar, and Archer on the other. Here, Archer looked a bigger man than he had at Scotland Yard that morning, perhaps because Lois was so short. She was sheet-white. Her dark eyes looked huge and luminous. The red of her lips was strangely artificial. She wore a pale blue smock which covered her from neck to knees, or just above the knees, but it wasn't shapeless; was drawn in at the waist enough to outline her figure. She did not appear to see Dawlish, who took in the whole scene at a glance, including another plainclothes detective who was at one side.

On the bar was an open box of chocolates.

A few blank spaces were among the rich dark pieces, which had a luscious appearance. Chocolates were almost irresistible to Felicity and these were her favourites, bought from a nearby shop where they made them in a kitchen at the rear.

Dawlish stopped just inside the room.

Archer said in a hard, accusing voice: 'Let's go over this again. You bought those chocolates yourself.'

'Yes! Mrs. Dawlish asked me to.'

'Why didn't she buy them herself?'

'Because I pass the Choc Shop on my way home, I often buy them for her.'

'Who paid for them?'

'I paid but they would go on the housekeeping bill. I've told you!'

Ordinary, everyday facts. Every word was the truth. One of the great attributes of Lois Kenning was that she would readily buy odds and ends for the kitchen when she went home or when she came to work. Ordinary, everyday facts which now had a touch of horror in them.

The Choc Shop had been a chance discovery of his, years ago. Oh, dear God.

Archer demanded in his hard and domineering voice: 'When did you buy those chocolates?'

'Yesterday afternoon, on the way home from work.'

'So you took them home?'

'Yes, I've told you I did. Yes! But I didn't open the box.'

'That's easy to say. It's tied up with ribbon, you could have untied it and tied it up again, couldn't you?'

'I could have,' she gasped, 'but I didn't!'

Dawlish wanted to help her. She was so distraught and under such terrible pressure, and he would have liked to ease that pressure, but – supposing he did? It was a hundred, it was a thousand to one that Archer was wrong and Lois knew nothing about the poisoning, but he could be right. To interfere unless he went far beyond the bounds of interrogation would be folly. Dawlish did not think she was aware of his presence yet, and could not be sure that Archer was.

Archer said: 'Now I want you to tell me all about those chocolates.'

'I've told you!' she cried.

'Please tell me again.' His voice was even, unemotional; the voice of a machine.

'I bought them yesterday afternoon at the Choc Shop. It's a homemade chocolate and confectionery shop in a turning off Victoria Street. Mrs. Dawlish wanted some, and asked me to buy them. I took them home and left them in my bag – I always bring a shopping bag with books and an apron and oddments in every day. I brought them here this morning. Mrs. Dawlish offered me one, but I refused.'

'Why did you buy them last night and not this morning?'

'It wasn't last night it was early afternoon. The shop isn't open when I come past in the mornings.'

'Why did you refuse Mrs. Dawlish's offer of one?' Archer's voice was still mechanical.

'I seldom eat chocolates!'

'Seldom? Or never?'

'Seldom – don't put words in my mouth.'

'Why don't you eat chocolates more often? Don't you like them?'

'I love them!'

'Then why don't you eat them more?'

'I don't want to get fat!'

'I see,' Archer said, indifferently. 'Now – what did you do with the chocolates this morning?'

'I put them on the bar – about where they are now.'

'Opened?'

'*No!* I've told you – I didn't open them.'

'What time was this?'

'I don't know exactly but it was soon after nine,' answered Lois. 'I was a little late. I'd seen Mr. Dawlish downstairs as I came in, and hurried straight up here. Mrs. Dawlish called out that she would be with me in a few minutes, and I was to carry on.'

Yes, thought Dawlish, some of this he knew to be true, all had a ring of truth in it. He felt as if a sword were turning in his heart, sending pain throughout his whole body. He had left Felicity so happy. They had had such a wonderful night. Such wonderful joy. Their shared fears had died. And she had slept late, then rushed to cook his breakfast so that he could face the day well fortified. Without make-up, wearing only that old dressing-gown, how good she had looked.

And now . . .

He could imagine her here, sick, writhing in pain.

He heard Archer again with his remorseless questioning. He had to be remorseless, he had to dig as deep as he could for the truth, so – he had to be cruel. As he, Patrick Dawlish had been cruel with people whom he had suspected of committing grave crimes. 'Nice' people did commit heinous crimes; often.

'What did you "carry on" with after Mrs. Dawlish called out?' Archer demanded.

'Vacuuming the passage and this room.'

'How long did that take?'

'I – I don't know.'

'How often have you done the work?' demanded Archer.

'Perhaps – perhaps six times.'

'Can't you estimate how long it takes?'

'It – it must be an hour.'

'An *hour* to push a vacuum cleaner round this flat!'

'Yes, easily!' Lois cried. 'By the time I've moved all the furniture and fitted on the nozzle for the corners and the furniture itself – yes, easily an hour, more likely an hour and a half!'

'Did Mrs. Dawlish come in?' Archer's flat voice was in sharp contrast to hers, now high-pitched and despairing.

'No, she . . .'

'Weren't you surprised?'

'Vaguely, but she – she sometimes takes it into her head to do the bedroom thoroughly and I thought that was what she was doing.'

'Why didn't you go and make sure?'

'It wasn't my business to go and ask her what she was up to!' cried Lois. 'She might be on the telephone, she might be resting for all I knew. I just went on doing my job.'

'Until when?' Archer wanted to know.

'Until eleven o'clock, when I went into the kitchen,' answered Lois, more steadily. 'Whether she's in or not I always have twenty minutes or so off at eleven o'clock, for coffee. She usually joins me when she's in.'

'Did she this morning?'

'No,' Lois answered, huskily. 'No. I expected she would be in the kitchen or would come soon, so I put the kettle on and got the tray ready.'

'Did you notice anything?' demanded Archer.

'I – I don't know what you mean.'

'Was anything different from when you'd left the kitchen?' asked Archer.

With a rush, she cried: 'Yes, the chocolates were open, two or three were gone. And I . . .'

Archer interrupted sharply: 'Did you take one?'

'*No, I seldom eat chocolates! I keep telling you.* I went and peeped into the bedroom to see if Mrs. Dawlish was lying down, but the bed wasn't even made. I simply couldn't understand it. I didn't know what to do, and then – *then* I heard a groan.'

'So,' said Archer, sarcasm thick in his voice. 'One and a half to one and three quarter hours after you had first missed her you heard Mrs. Dawlish groan. What did you do then?'

Lois Kenning's voice was now choky as she answered. 'I had not missed her, as you say. I simply hadn't seen her. What she does in her own home is her business, not mine. I went to the bathroom which leads off the bedroom and – and she was on the floor. She was obviously very ill. I called out to her but she didn't seem to realize I was there, and I knew at once she needed a doctor. I didn't know hers so I called the emergency – 999. Then I went back to her and sponged her forehead and tried to help, but she was in such pain and I couldn't really do anything. Thank heavens the police were here in five minutes and the doctor soon afterwards.'

'Yes,' said Archer. 'Yes, *someone* acted quickly. But you, Mrs. Kenning – are you aware that if you had found Mrs. Dawlish an hour, or even half an hour earlier you might have saved her life? Are you aware . . .'

Dawlish spoke for the first time, saying very quietly: 'She isn't dead yet, Chief Inspector.'

Archer spun round; so he hadn't realized that Dawlish was there.

And Lois turned, too, a pirouette of a movement, swift and graceful. Her face lit up. Her fear seemed to fade. She ran towards Dawlish and what she said took his breath away.

'Oh, Pat!' she cried. 'Thank God you're here!'

CHAPTER TEN

REPORT

'THEY were her very words, sir,' Chief Inspector Archer said to Commander Liddell, when they were together in the C.I.D. Chief's office. ' "Oh, Pat! Thank God you're here!" I've never been more taken aback, it was the last thing I expected, but if you'd heard her, sir, you wouldn't have been in any doubt. There's something between Mr. Dawlish and the Kenning woman. She absolutely flung herself into his arms, too.'

It was the middle of the same afternoon.

Archer had been back only half an hour, and on the commander's desk in a square office which had one wall of windows and three high and plain, was Archer's report: a brief preliminary one neatly typewritten. Archer was aware of the intense gaze from the muddy eyes, and thought as he had thought before: a lot of people likened Liddell to a bull, but he sometimes looked more like a big, fat frog.

'And how did Dawlish respond?' Liddell asked.

'He looked bloody embarrassed, couldn't get her off him quickly enough. He played it cool, though it was the woman who gave the game away.'

'Archer,' Liddell said, 'I'll want a lot of convincing that there is any game.'

'I don't think you would if you'd been present,' replied Archer. 'It's not certain of course and not proved but I'd like to work that angle. We've only got to prove that he's been seeing her clandestinely and it will be strong supporting evidence.'

'Follow it up,' Liddell approved.

'I will, sir!'

'What's the Kenning woman like to look at?'

'She's one of the most beautiful women I've ever seen,' Archer replied, without the slightest hesitation.

'My, my!'

'I'm not joking, sir. Southern European type, dark hair,

lovely face, all the curves – she's got a bosom that would make a thousand men leave home. She . . .' He hesitated, and then opened the report which was facing Liddell until he came to a photograph. It was a black and white enlargement of a snapshot, head and shoulders; and there was laughter in the dark eyes. Liddell studied it and said:

'Okay. She's a looker. Where did you get this?'

'In her handbag.'

'Hers? Get permission to search?'

'She didn't argue. I thought it just possible there would be some traces of powder – arsenic with luck! – or even a hypodermic needle. That's how the arsenic was put into the chocolates: injected with a hypodermic needle and then the chocolate was melted and smoothed over to hide the puncture.' Archer now sounded positively smug.

'You wouldn't be guessing, would you?'

'No, sir,' said Archer. 'I stood over old Ross in the lab just now and he pointed the marks out after I'd asked him if it could be done that way. He's going to let me know how many chocolates had arsenic in them; three did for certain: at least one that Mrs. Dawlish ate and two we examined up in the lab.'

'How is Mrs. Dawlish?' inquired Liddell.

'I called the hospital just before coming here, sir. They reported no change. We've a policewoman with her, of course, and the doctor promised to get in touch if there was the slightest change. A Dr. Tenby from the Westminster hospital,' Archer added.

'What are her chances?' Liddell wanted to know.

'No more than fifty-fifty.'

Liddell sat squat and solid at his desk, looking hard at the younger man. Archer had an ordinary face, a rather blotchy complexion, sandy-coloured hair; he was the kind of man who could easily get lost in a crowd. Not yet thirty-five, he was young for his rank even in these days of quick promotion at the Yard, and it would not be long before he became a superintendent. Liddell knew that his dull-looking exterior hid a bursting enthusiasm; that when he was questioning witnesses he could sound like a prosecuting counsel. He had a trick of nuance and another of using short sentences which put urgency into his questions, with more than a hint of aggressiveness.

'What about the Choc Shop?' Liddell asked.

'I've two men over there now. Mrs. Dawlish has been buying that particular kind of chocolate from there for years. Mr. Dawlish goes in for some occasionally, too. It's always the same variety – more strongly-flavoured than most.'

'What with?' Liddell barked.

'Can be coffee – liqueurs of different kinds – or nougats,' Archer replied.

'All strong enough to hide the flavour of arsenic,' Liddell remarked sagely. 'So anyone who knew the kind of chocolate Mrs. Dawlish liked knew where to get them and how to get her to eat the arsenic without the flavour being too noticeable.'

'Yes, sir.'

Liddell stood up, waved the other man to stay in his seat, and thrust his chin forward, making his lips look very thick; now he was more bull-like than like a frog. He rounded the desk and then sat against it, very close to Archer, a deliberate and dominating pose.

'You think there's been an *affaire* between Dawlish and the Kenning woman?'

'Yes.'

'You think between them they might have tried to murder Mrs. Dawlish to clear the road for themselves?'

'Yes,' Archer asserted, between clenched teeth.

'Well, keep it to yourself. Understand? Don't breathe a word about what you think to anyone else, whether it's to a copper or your wife – anyone. You haven't, have you?' Liddell barked.

'No, sir!'

'Then *don't*! Understand?'

'I – I wouldn't dream of it, sir.' Archer pressed against the back of the chair, feeling crowded, feeling almost as if it were difficult to breathe. But his gaze met Liddell's unwaveringly, until the commander moved round to the other side of the desk, and relaxed.

'Use all the men you want and keep me in close touch, hourly if needs be.'

'Right, sir.'

Liddell nodded, Archer got up from the wooden chair, stretching as if he had been cramped. He went out, closing the door quietly, and wiped his forehead before he moved along to the office he shared with five other chief inspectors. Once he sat at his desk, he felt much less oppressed. It would not have surprised him had Liddell told him he was talking out of the back of his neck, but the Old Man saw the possibility all right.

My God! What a case this could be – especially if Mrs. Dawlish died!

Dawlish heard the ring of the telephone, and went almost rigid, but relaxed enough to get up from his desk and answer. He had an instrument on the desk but few knew that number and he used it mostly for outgoing calls; the other telephone with three extensions was the home number: Felicity's more than his. And it was the number which Dr. Tenby would use, or anyone at the hospital. It rang under his hand before he lifted it.

'Dawlish,' he announced.

It could be word from Tenby.

A woman said in a distraught voice: 'Oh, Mr. Dawlish, I'm terribly sorry.'

It was Lois Kenning.

He hadn't seen or spoken to her since she had left the apartment with Archer and another policeman, an hour or so ago. It was now nearly four o'clock, so it was an hour and a half ago. So many things had happened that each seemed to be forgotten until something else happened to bring it sharply to mind again, but he had held the mental image of Lois clearly for much of the time. Even now he could see the way she looked – her enormous relief – when she realized he was in the apartment. He could hear her cry: 'Pat! Thank God you're here!' He could feel her body pressed against his and her arms about him – and he could recall the expression on Archer's face and be virtually sure what the detective had thought in that moment of time.

And here she was: distraught again.

He had a sense amounting to certainty that her 'terribly sorry' did not mean about Felicity but about the way she had behaved when she had seen him. He had to say something, and he said gruffly:

'I know. There's no change.'

'No . . .' she began, and then checked herself, so he knew

that he was right. 'I – I'm terribly sorry,' she repeated, but now it was an anti-climax. 'Not only about – about Mrs. Dawlish but about the way I behaved.'

'In your place, anyone would have been frightened,' he said.

There was a sound which was like a catch of breath, before she went on in a more controlled voice:

'You – you don't believe I – I had anything to do with it, do you?'

'Of course I don't,' Dawlish replied as positively as he could.

'Thank God for that!' she said, and for a few moments the only sound was of her heavy breathing.

There was a vehemence in her voice and manner which he could not fail to notice, and which was very strange. Vehemence? Yes – and intensity. It had been strongly in evidence when Archer had questioned her, and even at the beginning he had been surprised, expecting her to be calmer; but then, he did not know how long she had been under the relentless pressure which Archer had been exerting. It was as noticeable now as then and he did not really understand why, unless it were simply that she was under great strain, perhaps suffering from shock not only because she had found Felicity, but because Archer had made it obvious that he suspected her; or at least, that she was a suspect.

'Lois,' he said, 'it's inane to say "don't worry about it" but there's no need to worry about the policeman's suspicion. You were an obvious possibility and he chose his favourite way of trying to break you down. In the circumstances you stood up to him remarkably well, and you really needn't worry.'

She said: 'I'm not worried about myself, truly.'

'And it isn't any use worrying about my wife,' Dawlish said flatly.

'I – I wasn't thinking only of her, either,' Lois replied. 'I'm desperately worried about you.'

'You know, there really isn't any need . . .' began Dawlish.

'Oh, God!' she exclaimed. 'Oh, God! You don't know, do you? You haven't any idea.'

Abruptly, she rang off.

He could hear the echo of her voice, the desperation in it:

'Oh, God! You don't know, do you? You haven't any idea.'
Throughout his life he had heard men and women speaking
in that same tone, and desperation was the only word he
could think of. He had known women call and plead for his
help and win it, eventually, because of that same form of
vehemence. Whenever he heard it, some chord was struck
within him, and his impulse was to go and find out what was
causing the trouble: to go and help.

There was more than that, now.

The impulse to help was still there, of course, but there
was another stronger, near-magnetic impulse. He needed to
find out why she was in such a mood because the knowledge
might help him to find out what had happened here in this
apartment.

She *might* know more than she had admitted.

He was too much of a policeman to reject that possibility,
at least until she had been checked for possible motives,
for . . .

The telephone bell rang again.

His mind was so attuned to Felicity that again he thought
it might be from the hospital, and he was afraid to answer.
But that was madness; he had to answer, quickly. That was
why he was here, why he could not stir from this apartment.
He was awaiting word from the hospital. So he plucked up
the receiver, and said:

'Dawlish.'

A man in a toneless voice said with awful positiveness:
'Now there's only one of you left.'

And the man rang off.

Dawlish stood over the end of the big couch with the
receiver clutched in his hands, knuckles strained white, jaws
clamped together. A faint buzz came from the instrument
but that was the only sound. It was an age before he replaced
the receiver, an age before that voice faded in his ears. In
fact it did not fade completely, he sensed that it would
always be droning faintly at the back of his mind until he
could identify the man, and the threat was completely removed.

It was almost as if he knew that Felicity was dead.

She couldn't be, could she? She couldn't be!

Dawlish could sit and wait no longer, he had to find out at
once. He picked up the receiver and dialled the hospital. The

operator had a trick of sounding patient and sympathetic, always a help, and she recognized him immediately so that he was put through to the ward sister without delay. The sister had a rich, deep voice; he thought she was Jamaican.

'Your wife is more comfortable, Mr. Dawlish. Dr. Tenby said he would come and see her again in the next half-hour and call you if the improvement was maintained.' After a pause, she asked in an unflurried voice: 'Are you there, Mr. Dawlish?'

'Yes,' he said gruffly. 'Yes. Thank you. I'll stay here – at my apartment – until he's called.'

'I'll see that he gets the message,' the ward sister promised.

Dawlish felt the first lift of heart he had known since he had come home, the first real cause for hope and the certainty that the man who had telephoned had no real knowledge of Felicity's condition. "More comfortable" – thank God! He sat on the couch for a few minutes, with his eyes closed, then sprang to his feet and moved more briskly than he had for hours. Slowly, he became aware of a hollow feeling in his stomach.

'My lord!' he exclaimed. 'I'm hungry!'

He hadn't eaten since the breakfast Felicity had cooked for him! He could recall that meal and Felicity without the doom-like weight on his mind, and he went briskly into the kitchen, put on a kettle, found bread and butter and cheese and ate heartily while sitting up at the bar. The *Daily Globe* was there, folded to the article *Should We Keep Our Coppers At Home?* He read the article again, and on the whole liked it. Mr. Edgar Rapp, in this guise at least, was not taking sides.

Never trust a man who *said* he wasn't taking sides.

Dawlish's mind began to work more freely until in turn he began to feel the stirring of anger and resentment and frustration, all the emotions he had known when he had walked at that furious pace from 'old' New Scotland Yard. He would never recapture that mood again, the seething anger coupled with a sense of helplessness; what he felt now was but an echo of it.

Suddenly, a simple fact struck him, as heavily and painfully as if he had been struck by a brick.

He wasn't going back to the office; he was no longer Deputy Assistant Commissioner Dawlish; that long and rewarding period in a full life was over. It was hard to believe, and momentarily, he wondered whether he had been crazy to be so impetuous, but before long his mood hardened and he knew that Frazer and Lane virtually set out to emasculate him in the job. He had taken the only attitude possible.

He felt sure of that, had no sense of doubt at all, when the front door bell rang. Policemen were outside, screening him, so this wouldn't be a newspaper or a casual caller, it would be someone in authority or on business.

He opened the door.

Sir Charles Frazer stood there, hat in hand, bald head reflecting the light.

CHAPTER ELEVEN

PLEA FOR PATIENCE

BEHIND Frazer was a policeman.

At the door was a youthful-looking man with rimless glasses, who appeared only for a moment before a police hand descended on his shoulder and the owner of the hand said in a gargantuan whisper:

'You've been told *no*.'

Dawlish, vaguely aware of the byplay outside, also vaguely aware that the youth was a newspaperman, stood aside as he said in a flat voice: 'Good afternoon, Commissioner.' Frazer came into the passage, and followed Dawlish to the big room. Tight-lipped and hard-eyed as he was, Dawlish was not at that moment an easy man to talk to.

Frazer turned to face him.

'Dawlish,' he said, 'I came primarily to say how very sorry I am about the attempt on your wife's life.'

Primarily? wondered Dawlish. 'You are very kind,' he said formally. 'Will you sit down?' He indicated a corner of the big couch, and Frazer sank into it as gracefully as the softness would allow.

'In fact the news about your wife tipped the scales. I was vacillating between coming to see you and hoping you would come to see me.'

'I didn't think we had anything left to discuss,' Dawlish said stiffly.

'I have a request to make,' replied Frazer. 'Both officially and personally.' When Dawlish did not speak, he went on very bluntly: 'I want you to withdraw your resignation.'

Without hesitation, Dawlish said: 'I can't imagine anything that would make me.'

'Your going will mean a very serious loss to the police force, it will make an already difficult task even more difficult and it can only harm the police force in London, in the country, and throughout the world. It is much more than a matter of personal outrage. The report which you gave me makes this clear. I know you are outraged, I understand why and I see much justification. If it would help I have no doubt the chairman of the committee will extend his sincere apologies for his failure to consult you. So would Lane. And so do I.'

'Nice of you,' Dawlish said again, mechanically.

One thing was very clear: someone very high up had been told of the resignation and had given instructions: make him withdraw it. Someone, conceivably the Home Secretary himself, knew that over the years Dawlish had become a popular figure with the general public, that his resignation would not be taken calmly but had all the ingredients of a sensation. And no one who knew him could doubt that he would talk freely to the newspapers if he believed that could help to change the official policy. Frazer was here to repair the damage which he and Lane had done that morning, and whatever his private thoughts he was making a handsome attempt.

'I hope you will accept such apologies and continue as if there had been no conflict,' said Frazer. Then a gleam of apprehension showed in his eyes and he asked in a sharper voice: 'You've told no one, have you?'

'Not yet,' Dawlish answered.

'Then the damage can be repaired.'

'Not so easily,' Dawlish replied, but he relaxed a little and picked up a silver box of cigarettes and proffered it; when Frazer said 'No thanks, I don't smoke,' Dawlish took a cigarette and lit it from a match from a box marked: *Schweiz Hotel, Zurich*. As he doused the flame in a stone ashtray he went on: 'I haven't had much time to think. I ran into the situation here within a quarter of an hour of leaving you. But what thinking I have done suggests I can help the police here and abroad better by resigning and telling the world why, than by coming back.'

'I don't agree with you,' Frazer said.

'By police I don't mean the police establishment in the sense of its administrative leaders,' said Dawlish. 'I mean the police who do the hard, often unrewarding work in the field. You've asked for more money with which to protect the public against crime. The Home Office says that it can only be found if stringent economies are made elsewhere, and I doubt if my branch was the only one to feel the axe.' He paused long enough for Frazer to comment but when no word was forthcoming, he went on: 'This kind of policy has been followed in Westminster from the time we first had a police force. It's been a case of too few policemen and too little money all the time. I think that any kind of economy in the war against crime is short-sighted and dangerous, and could be deadly. As a private individual I can say all this. As a Deputy Assistant Commissioner, I can't, without creating problems all round. So the simple way is to act and speak as a private individual who has more background knowledge than most.'

After a long pause, Frazer remarked: 'You certainly have that.'

Dawlish made no comment, but drew on his cigarette, let the smoke out in a cloud, and then put the cigarette out. It was weeks since he had smoked at all, and his mouth felt dry, with a slight unpleasant taste.

'Dawlish,' said Frazer, 'I believe we should all speak with one voice.'

'How can we, if we think different ways?'

Frazer didn't answer.

Dawlish wondered what manner of man he really was; whether he was actually as conventional as Lane but able to present himself more effectively; whether he was trustworthy, a man to rely on once his word was given. And – was he a policeman at heart? One great bone of contention among the professional police was that non-professionals were too often put in charge of them, and while this was less true than it had once been it was still true enough.

He, Dawlish, was an "amateur"!

Frazer had been in the Colonial Civil Service before his present appointment.

He broke a long silence, abruptly.

'I shall ask a favour, Dawlish. I hope you can see your way to granting it.' To put the matter in those terms must have been a considerable effort, and Dawlish warmed a little towards the man, while knowing that asking for a favour meant that he was desperately anxious to get his own way.

'If I possibly can,' Dawlish said.

'Thank you. Will you say nothing about your resignation to anyone for an agreed period – one week from today, say.

This will give you time to consider fully and also to recover from the shock of what happened to your wife. And it will give me and the others time to study reports and to reflect more deeply. It will also allow time for you – if you will be so good – to put in your request for more funds and to submit the request with a reasoned memorandum.' When Dawlish did not immediately answer, Frazer went on with tension growing in his voice: 'In other words, postpone the resignation for one week.'

Dawlish thought again: 'He's really desperately anxious. I wonder who's been after him?' And he thought: 'I mustn't keep him on a hook too long or he'll get mad. He smiled and said pleasantly:

'I'll gladly say yes, but for one thing.'

'What thing?'

'I can't promise to withdraw or appear to minimize anything I said in Zurich.'

'I shall rely on your discretion,' said Frazer with an expression which showed his great relief. He took a folded paper from his pocket; in fact there proved to be two papers, one Dawlish's note of resignation and the other a photo-copy of it. 'In order that there can never be any doubt and no need for immediate formal action, I suggest you write: "Suspended for one week from today", on both copies and I acknowledge receipt on both copies. Does that seem satisfactory?'

'Perfectly,' Dawlish said, and he took out a pen.

He also felt a tremendous surge of relief. He did not try to justify that or to explain it; he simply acknowledged the fact as he wrote the single sentence, signed and dated it, the relief was like a physical thing. His heart was as light as it could be, and he actually forgot Felicity for a few seconds.

'I hope very much that your wife continues to improve,' said Frazer, as they shook hands at the door. 'And I have personally spoken to Commander Liddell who is in charge of the investigation, instructing him to exert himself and his men in every way to find out who was responsible. I've made it clear that I expect results very quickly.'

'You're very good,' Dawlish said. 'Thank you, sir. Goodbye.'

He closed the front door on Frazer, catching a glimpse of the policemen but seeing no sign of the fair-haired man with the rimless glasses. He went back to the big room, the mood of relief still very strong. If he had to resign a week from now then it would be only after deep reflection, and he had a chance now to fight for what he wanted without being in immediate conflict with the Home Office. It might only be an armistice but during it he could do a great deal to strengthen his case.

And thank God, Felicity was improving!

He stepped to his desk and used the private line telephone to call his office, then realized it was after half past five: Childs had probably left. But no, Childs, who should not really have been there but was as trustworthy a man as Dawlish knew, answered the call.

'Deputy Assistant Commissioner Dawlish's office,' he said.

'It's good to hear you again,' said Dawlish.

'And it is good to hear you, sir,' declared Childs, with more expression in his voice than Dawlish could remember. 'How is Mrs. Dawlish?'

'More comfortable.'

'I can't tell you how glad I am, sir,' said Childs, the warmth still in his voice. 'And I speak for everyone on the staff here. There is a great deal of concern.'

'You're all very good,' Dawlish said, almost humbly. '*Very* good. You know that Archer is in charge of the investigation, don't you?'

'Yes,' said Childs, with noticeably less enthusiasm. 'I suppose it was inevitable, and we couldn't use one of our own teams.'

'Won't theirs be better?' asked Dawlish, and when Childs didn't reply immediately he asked with a touch of apprehension in his voice: 'What's wrong, Jim?'

'We – ell,' responded Childs slowly, 'I don't know that anything is actually wrong, but when Gordon Scott saw Archer and offered to help – I suggested that, sir – Archer sent him back with a flea in his ear. I would have thought that such an occurrence would have thawed the ice between here and the new building, but if that was anything to judge by, the ice is even thicker. Would you have expected it?'

Dawlish pondered before he said: 'No. No, I wouldn't. I must have trodden on more corns than I'd realized.' In fact he could understand it to some degree, it would be considered a matter of departmental pride, even honour. He pondered again before adding: 'Let them handle it for the time being. If any need arises I'll take a hand myself, we won't use Gordon'. He held on to the telephone, frowning, staring at a photograph of Felicity on the wall above the desk. 'Jim,' he went on, 'were you with us when Lois Kenning started work here, at the flat?'

'I don't even know the name,' replied Childs.

'I gave the office details of her name and address. Ask around and find out if she *was* ever screened,' Dawlish said. 'They might have been waiting for my specific instructions.'

'I'll check at once, and I'll call you back,' promised Childs. 'Before I go, sir . . .'

'Yes?'

'Did everything go all right this morning with the Commissioner?'

'It couldn't have gone much worse,' answered Dawlish. 'Keep that under your hat, and have the report you gave me extended. I'm going to have to present a very strong case to save us from having to cut running costs.'

'Here?' Again Child's voice rose upwards in the kind of emotional reaction he would never have permitted himself before his retirement. 'Why, we run on a shoestring!'

'I know that but not everybody does,' Dawlish replied. 'And it isn't only what we spend, they seem to have some doubts about our being worth while. One other thing,' he went on before Childs could gasp out a protest at that statement. 'Write a letter from me to you, asking you to come back on a temporary service basis for an indeterminate period, will you? And let me have a formal letter of agreement.'

'I will indeed,' promised Childs. 'What a lot of so-and-so's VIPs can be!'

Dawlish rang off, more grateful that he could say that Child's had turned up when he had; he, Dawlish, now felt much more free to act as he thought fit, and to be away from the office as often as necessary. His problem was what to do for the best effect. It was disquieting that Archer had been so brusque with Gordon Scott, but he saw no more than a further indication of deteriorating relationship between his branch and the main force of the Criminal Investigation Department. He could not take it for granted that all was well with Felicity but it was surprising how much more free he felt to concentrate on the actual work. In a way it was a good thing that Archer was looking after the investigation into the poisoning.

He hadn't yet told Archer about the afternoon's telephone call. He dialled the Yard, but Archer was out, so he left a message with a sergeant, and then went into the kitchen and read yet again the brief article by Edgar Rapp.

Should We Keep Our Coppers At Home?

Despite some glib optimism from certain of its delegates, the seventeenth International Police Conference broke up in Zurich yesterday on a note of deep gloom.

Many delegates admitted that they doubted whether it would ever become an effective force.

One or two even doubted whether as an organization it will ever meet again.

The reason for all this gloom? Shortage of money.

That really isn't surprising when one realizes that most civilized [sic!] countries and big cities spend a fortune fighting crime. Or, as I have heard it put, failing to fight crime.

If the governments and the civic authorities won't spend enough to keep crime off their own doorsteps, how can one expect them to finance a battle against crime which takes place across the English Channel, across the Atlantic, or on the other side of the world?

'Keep one's coppers at home' is a slogan one might hear loud and clear from many sources and many climes in the next few weeks.

And a question will doubtless be asked:

'Are we our brother's jailers?'

Dawlish put the newspaper down and said quietly: 'I want to talk to this man.' He was near an extension telephone at the end of the couch so he dialled the number of the *Daily Globe*, 23610121, to get a brisk answer and:

'I'll put you through to the news desk.'

A moment later, a man said: 'Ed's half-expected any time, but he may not be in all night. Who wants him?'

'My name is Dawlish,' Dawlish answered. 'Patrick Dawlish.'

There was a gasp, clearly of astonishment, a pause which did not last very long, and then the speaker said:

'You're probably nearer him than I am – he's been trying to get an interview with you all day. He's a little chap, fair-haired, who wears rimless glasses. You shouldn't have any difficulty in picking him out of the crowd of newspapermen howling at your door.' Then in a sudden change of tone the speaker dropped his flippant manner, and went on: 'I'm very sorry to hear about your wife, sir. We had a report from the hospital only half an hour ago, though: she was showing signs of improvement. Everyone here is very glad.'

All Dawlish could say in a husky voice was: 'Thank you.'

CHAPTER TWELVE

ED RAPP

THE two policemen who had been on the landing below Dawlish's flat and the lifts were still there, a big man and a thin one of medium height. When Dawlish described Edgar Rapp, the big man answered without hesitation: 'Oh, he's here all right,' and went on with a laugh: 'He's tried more ways of getting to see you than a cat has lives. Do you really want to see him?'

'I'd rather his brothers-in-print didn't know – but yes,' answered Dawlish.

'I'm sure we can arrange it,' said the big policeman, and he turned towards the lift. Before a car had come up, however, the door to the staircase, marked with a red sign *Emergency Exit,* opened and the youthful-looking man with the rimless glasses stepped through.

'*Did* I hear aright?' he asked, holding his breath in mock astonishment.

Dawlish could not resist a chuckle, and even the big policeman grinned.

'If you can spare me a few minutes,' Dawlish said.

'I don't believe it,' said Rapp. 'No one doubted the wholesomeness of manna from heaven but I doubt the honesty of this invitation!' He went to the open door and darted quickly inside as if afraid that Dawlish would change his mind.

Dawlish took him into the big room. He was older than he seemed from a distance, with crows' feet at his eyes and mouth; it was his flaxen hair and the look of astonishment which the glasses gave him which created the illusion of youthfulness – that and the fact that he was not more than five feet two or three in height, and had a boyish, rather spindly figure.

'May I sit on the spot warmed by the Commissioner?' he asked.

'There.' Dawlish pointed. 'What will you have to drink?'

'A whisky-and-soda, if I may.' Behind the lenses pale grey eyes glistened and Rapp followed Dawlish's every movement as he crossed to a carved oak cabinet in a corner which opened to reveal bottles and glasses, the way he opened the bottles and poured out, carrying a generous tot and a soda syphon to Rapp, who filled the glass nearly up to the brim. Dawlish mixed his drink weak, too. 'Cheers.'

'Cheers.'

They sipped.

'Mr. Dawlish,' Rapp said. 'I'm sorry about your wife.'

'Thank you. She's making progress.'

'I'm glad. Do you know the man in charge of the investigation?'

'Chief Inspector Archer, yes.'

'He is extremely cautious in what he says to the Press.'

'So he should be.'

'Do you know why your wife was poisoned?' demanded Rapp.

'No.'

'Are you going to take any part in the investigation yourself?'

'I doubt it,' Dawlish said. 'It is difficult to be objective where your own family is concerned.'

'*Is* it true both you and your wife had threatening letters?'

'It is true that Mr. Archer is in full control of the investigation and will tell the Press everything he wants them to know. Why do you hate the police, Mr. Rapp?'

Rapp, in the middle of putting his glass to his lips, was so surprised that he nearly spilled some of his drink. His eyes glistened with real or false indignation, and he sat more upright.

'*I* don't hate the police.'

'Your article in today's *Globe* wasn't exactly full of admiration for them.'

Rapp stared at him for what seemed a long time, drank more deeply, placed the glass near the stone ashtray, and slowly shook his head. There was something bird-like about him as he said:

'I don't believe you misread it like that.'

'*Mis*read?'

'My article,' said Rapp, with dignity, 'was a deeply considered piece written in basic English to draw the public's attention to the fact that the police get a raw deal, money-wise. It was also intended to draw attention to the fact that you, the glamour boy of the police of Great Britain, if I may put it that way, a giant in the war against crime, were having your hands tied behind your back because the International Police Conference hasn't enough money to bless itself with.' He peered more closely at Dawlish and went on pleadingly: 'Tell me you didn't misread it! Tell me you *are* only bluffing.'

Dawlish said drily: 'It could have been read two ways, and you could have had your tongue in your cheek.'

'*That* I admit,' conceded Rapp. 'Tell me, did it hurt?'

'Did what hurt?'

'The wigging from the Commissioner?'

Stony-faced, Dawlish replied. 'Do all newspapermen guess as wildly as you?'

'There's a difference between a guess and intelligent deduction,' Rapp protested. 'The Home Office's troubleshooter and the Commissioner, who was brought in to help bring down expenses, not to increase them, didn't come here to slap your back, did they?'

'They came to my office for consultations,' Dawlish declared.

'And you stalked out and left them standing – I know, I followed you,' Rapp told him. 'Mighty and terrible you appeared in your wrath. I have never been so pleased. I've had a special hate for Lane since he axed three of the Home Office Press Department because they were newspapermen first and civil servants afterwards. From the way you looked, there was a most unholy row. I could have come to see you right away but you ran into the shocking situation with your wife.' Rapp paused, took another drink, and went on very quietly: 'I needn't use all you tell me, and won't use anything you say is off the record, but if I'm to be of any help I need to know the truth. I really do.'

Dawlish studied him thoughtfully.

Most newspapermen were wholly trustworthy if told something in confidence, but he didn't know Rapp well enough to be sure whether he could rely on him. In any case, he did not see why, at this stage, he should tell the man anything off the record. Yet there was something likeable about the man with his perky way and his casual manner; Dawlish certainly did not want to make an enemy of him.

So he said: 'I don't think it's any secret that the Commissioner and Sir Arbuthnot Lane came to tell me they want to allocate my branch less money, not more. And ...' he grinned, an amused and attractive grin – 'there isn't much doubt that they know I'm a difficult man to handle, a kind of rogue policeman, if you like, who does not share their reverence for the proper channels. They thought if they summoned me to their parlours enterprising newspapermen would make a lot of it and I might take the huff, whereas if they came to me, I might be in a more amenable mood.'

'Were you?' flashed Rapp.

'If telling them I thought that any branch of the police force home or abroad was the last thing we needed to economize on, that economies in the fight against crime was a kind of social suicide in which the English have been indulging for over two hundred years – no, I wasn't.'

Rapp's eyes lit up. 'Rogue cop,' he breathed. 'Social suicide with historical background. Beautiful!'

Dawlish smiled but without the same freedom.

'Call me one if you like but don't quote me. Quote me as saying that saving money on crime is a form of social suicide but don't quote me as saying it to my chief.'

'Nice distinction! What else may I quote you as saying?'

'That I don't believe any delegate in Zurich told you or anyone else that he thought that might be the last conference,' said Dawlish. 'It won't be. But the organization now known as the International Police Conference has to do more than limp along on what the regular police forces can squeeze from their budgets. It needs to become a powerful and effective force in its own right.'

He was warming to the subject when the telephone bell rang.

He was startled both by the bell and by the fact that he had been so absorbed in what he was saying that he wished the caller anywhere but at the end of the line. Next instant, he realized that it might be about Felicity, and he sprang up, moved to the table where the telephone stood and snatched up the receiver.

'Dawlish.' It was almost a growl.

'This is Childs,' Childs said, quietly. 'I'm sorry I'm so late, but I've been checking all the records. Mrs. Kenning, Lois Kenning, wasn't screened by us or by anyone. We've no record in the department of her being in your employ at all.'

Dawlish said: 'Ask Records at the new building whether they know anything about her.'

'I will,' promised Childs, 'although . . .'

'What?'

'Archer's bound to have checked Records.'

'Let's just make sure,' said Dawlish. He looked up from the telephone to Rapp, and went on quietly: 'Do you know whether the Choc Shop has been investigated yet?'

'I know Archer's been there and that he left two men to keep at the job,' said Childs.

'Good.' Dawlish hesitated, then asked: 'When are you going home?'

'I'm in no hurry,' Childs assured him. 'If there's any news before I go, shall I call you at the flat?'

'Please,' answered Dawlish, and rang off.

From this angle, Rapp looked more like a little old man than a boy; the angle of light made his crows' feet seem deeper and darker, and his eyes had darker shadows. He watched Dawlish move back to the couch without speaking; either he was thinking deeply or he expected Dawlish to make some comment. There was something strange in his manner; one could almost call it repellent.

'Another whisky-and-soda?' asked Dawlish roughly.

'No,' said Rapp. 'I'm not much of a drinker.' He stood up. 'I ought to be on my way, sir. I don't want to miss tomorrow's early editions. I won't say a word you've asked me not to. Would you like me to read over any quotes from the office?'

After a moment's hesitation, Dawlish said: 'No thanks. I'll leave it to you.'

'Thank you. One other thing,' said Rapp.

'Yes?'

'Would you be prepared to write a signed article for us about the International Police Conference?'

Slowly, Dawlish answered: 'I don't see why not.'

'I have a feeling the editor would give his right arm for one,' declared Rapp. 'Don't be at all surprised if you get a call from him.'

'I won't,' promised Dawlish.

He saw the other man to the door, and turned back into the apartment, very puzzled and a little apprehensive. Something he had said over the telephone had affected the newspaperman, whose whole attitude had changed, and who couldn't get away quickly enough. And it wasn't yet seven o'clock, there was plenty of time to write his story for the first editions.

Why was he in such a hurry?

With a sudden swift movement, Dawlish downed his whisky-and-soda, and strode back towards the door. He could not be more than a minute behind the *Globe* reporter, might well catch him up. The two policemen were still in the hall and the large one pressed the lift bell in anticipation.

'Thanks,' Dawlish said. 'Don't you two ever go off duty?'

The smaller man said. 'Another two hours.'

'I hope they go fast for you!' Dawlish heard the lift draw up and saw the doors open and stepped inside. At night it was invariably a speedy journey both up and down, as all the office floors were empty. He did not stop at the street level foyer but went down to the garage, where he kept his car and Felicity kept hers – a sturdy Morris 1800. His was an easily recognizable Aston Martin.

Her car was in its usual place, easy to drive on to the ramp.

He went straight to it, taking out his keys: he had an ignition key to her car, as she had one to his. Thank God the news was hopeful! He started the engine, revved hard, and roared up the ramp which fed into one side of the main carriageway approach.

An M.G. with an open top was just moving off, and the lamplight shone on the flaxen hair of the *Globe* man.

'Got him!' Dawlish exulted.

Rapp turned right, on to the Embankment, and Dawlish, feeling secure from recognition, followed him without glancing at the half-dozen reporters and policemen still on duty outside. The police would not be interested in who was leaving the building ...

Wouldn't they, though!

Another car, a Rover, turned in his wake, and the odds were that a plainclothes man was at the wheel. Dawlish had a strange sensation: that he was being followed as a suspect by the police. He shrugged the thought off, yet it kept returning. He could not understand why Archer should arrange to have him followed.

Rapp turned left, at Battersea Bridge; so did Dawlish; and so did the Rover.

Before long, Rapp was driving among a warren of streets near Battersea Park, an area with which he had only a slight acquaintance. He thought that Rapp probably knew he was being followed by now but the newspaperman showed no sign of wanting to throw him off the scent. Instead, he pulled up at a corner house of two streets of three-storey buildings, parked the car and went up the stone steps leading to the front door.

Dawlish drove round the corner.

He was suddenly, acutely alarmed, for in two doorways he saw men, almost certainly police officers, watching that corner house. The Rover passed by, the driver obviously content to hand over to the watching men. Then Dawlish saw a third man at the wheel of a car just round the corner, and at the same moment saw the name of the street on a nameplate on a wall of the corner house.

It was Dander Street.

On the instant he remembered hearing Felicity and Lois talking, and Lois saying: '48, Dander Street, Battersea. If I walk over the bridge I can get a bus right to the door.'

The police were watching Lois Kenning, which was not surprising.

But why had Edgar Rapp, shrewd and knowledgeable Fleet Street man, rushed from Dawlish's home to see her?

CHAPTER THIRTEEN

DECLARATION

DAWLISH had not the slightest idea why he had been followed; not the slightest idea that he was suspected of having
an *affaire* with Lois Kenning. He was not only puzzled but
acutely anxious to find out what was going on. It was a long
time since he had become involved in the investigation of a
crime not connected with the Crime Haters, but the burning
personal issues in this case made it easy to forget that.

He was going into this house to find out what Rapp
wanted with Lois Kenning. The fact that the police would
see him go seemed a help rather than a hindrance.

He parked the car with swift, skilful manoeuvres and
strode back to the corner. He was moving and thinking with
the speed, which, over the years, had bewildered both the
police and criminals – without hesitation and with absolute
confidence. A part of his mind absorbed situations and places
with photographic accuracy, and although he had never
been here before the fact that he had driven past gave it all a
kind of familiarity. He reached the corner and swung round
and up the steps. He did not quite know what he would do
if he found the door locked, but he pushed it and it
opened.

He stepped inside a dimly lit passage.

Somewhere, a baby cried.

Somewhere, a woman called: 'Who is that?'

At once, Rapp answered: 'I won't keep you long.'

Now Dawlish was becoming accustomed to the light, and
the layout of the house; there were tens of thousands like it
in London. One narrow staircase led upwards, with narrow
landings, and a door by the side of the staircase showed that
there was a flat on the ground floor; each floor was probably
a self-contained flat, although the upper floors might be let
off in rooms.

He went swiftly up the stairs.

He heard Lois say: 'Who *are* you?'

'I'm from the *Daily Globe*,' Rapp said, 'and I want to help Mr. Dawlish as much as you do.'

Lois caught her breath, audibly.

Now Dawlish was at the first landing, which was also dimly lit. A passage led straight along from the head of the stairs to a closed door, while another passage led in the opposite direction, wall on one side, banister rail on the other. Dawlish pressed close against the wall, where he was less likely to be seen. A piece of furniture, cupboard or wardrobe, stood between him and the doorway where Rapp stood – at the end of the second passage.

Dawlish reached the shelter of the cupboard.

The layout of this floor was very clear now. Beyond the cupboard was the door at which the others stood, Rapp just inside the passage and in sight, Lois's shadow cast upon the wall behind him. There was a small landing and, beyond this, another flight of stairs. From the rooms above came the sound of the baby, crying.

Then Lois said: 'I've nothing to say to you.'

'All I want is to help Dawlish,' hissed Rapp.

He sounded sincere. He made no attempt to push past into the room, and when Dawlish put his head round the cupboard he saw him, in profile, light from the room shimmering on those glasses. He could hear Lois's heavy breathing.

She said: 'Oh God, if only I could!'

'If you tell me all you know, we can help him between us,' Rapp insisted.

How could they help? What did he mean? These questions surged through Dawlish's mind and he became aware of a secondary factor only vaguely: the intensity with which Lois had said: 'Oh God, if only I could!'

'I tell you we *can*,' insisted Rapp. 'And I can help you.'

She didn't answer.

'You know you're the number one suspect, don't you?' Rapp went on. 'There are at least three policemen watching this house and you're followed wherever you go. I tell you you're in trouble, deep trouble, and you need help badly. *Desperately.*'

After a long pause, she said: 'You'd better come in.'

She went inside and Rapp followed and the door closed; Dawlish heard a single click.

He moved from his hiding place soundlessly. There was light at the bottom and the sides of the door and he could hear voices but could not distinguish what was being said. His mind absorbed all that had passed between Rapp and Lois, and Rapp was certainly right and she was a suspect, perhaps the chief and only one, and she needed help, but – why did she think he, Dawlish, also needed help?

Because of the threats?

Had Felicity told her about the cryptic note and the telephone call? It was possible but even if she had, how did Rapp know?

He took the handle of the door between his fingers.

That one click had been when it had closed but was it self-locking? In this dim light he could not tell. He clasped and turned. In these old houses, the inside rooms usually had to be locked with a key, but a lot of people had Yale or similar locks fixed.

The handle turned. The door opened.

What *luck*, thought Dawlish, and he pushed the door very slowly, opening it only just wide enough to hear what was being said.

At that precise moment Chief Inspector Archer stepped out of a car in Dander Street, fifty yards away from the house where Dawlish stood. Two of Archer's men approached, and the three big fellows stood blocking the pavement, while others watched Number 48 from different points of vantage. Archer, who had left his wife and children in the middle of the family's evening meal when he had received the call from *Information,* asked briskly:

'Is he still here?'

'Yes, sir.' The spokesman was a man ten years his senior, a detective sergeant named Snow.

'How long's he been inside?'

'Six or seven minutes,' Snow answered. 'He parked round the corner and almost ran to Number 48, went up the steps and straight in.'

'Did he have a key?' demanded Archer.

'If he didn't, the door was unlocked.'

'People often have one dangling on a piece of string behind the letter-box,' a second man remarked.

Archer ignored him, and asked: 'Did the newspaperman Rapp get here first?'

'Only just,' Snow said. 'He'd hardly parked his car before Mr. Dawlish arrived, and I wouldn't have been surprised at a bit of a rumpus, Mr. Dawlish looked ready to break someone's neck.'

'Have we a man inside?'

'Yes,' answered Snow. 'I sent him in straight after Mr. Dawlish. I hope that was right, sir.'

'Quite right,' Archer assured him.

What he couldn't be sure was what to do next.

Although in his own mind he was now quite certain that Dawlish and the Kenning woman were having an *affaire*, he did not see where the newspaperman came in, and he had a healthy respect for reporters, while this particular one was known to be more acid-penned than most. He had little doubt that Dawlish had followed Rapp and, finding him here, wanted to know what he, Rapp, had learned.

If Rapp knew about a liaison, he would immediately suspect the motive for the attack on Mrs. Dawlish. It would have nothing to do with the phoney threats, anyone could write letters to themselves; it would have to do with getting her out of the way and leaving the road clear for Dawlish and the Kenning woman.

Obviously, they might be involved together.

As obviously, the Kenning woman might have poisoned the chocolates, so as to force Dawlish's hand.

Either way, an astute Fleet Street man would be alert to the possibilities and if he said as much or even allowed the others to suspect what he believed, he could be in danger. Archer, while facing this, did not believe that Dawlish could be unaware that the house was watched: that was one of the puzzling factors. On balance, Archer decided that Rapp was not in danger; further, that he could be questioned afterwards, and probably made to explain what had been said between them in the house.

And the police did have a man inside.

'We'll wait,' he decided. 'But we'll have the street door open and a couple of men very close by so that they can get inside the place quickly. I'll draw my car up nearer the house and wait in there,' he added.

'Right!' said Snow, and then remarked: 'It's a funny kettle of fish, isn't it?'

Archer snorted.

Dawlish stood still and silent by the door which was open only a crack.

He heard sounds which might have been of Lois, crying, but no voices. He had asked himself the same questions over and over again, but come up with no satisfactory answers.

How did Rapp think she could help him, Dawlish?

Why should either of them think he needed the kind of help they could possibly give him?

At last, Lois said in a husky voice: 'Oh, I'm sorry.'

'It's all right,' Rapp responded. 'Take your time.'

'I look so terrible when I cry.'

'Nothing could make you look terrible.'

She gave a funny little laugh. 'That's very gallant.'

'You are the kind of woman who brings out the best in a man,' declared Rapp. 'Can I get you something?'

'No, I'm all right. I am, really. Or I will be in a minute. How – how well do you know him?'

'Patrick Dawlish? I doubt if anyone but his wife knows him and I wouldn't like to be sure about her,' Rapp responded. 'He looks all brawn and no brain but if there's a better mind in the police force, I've yet to come in contact with it. He can look an idiot, behave like a fluffy sheepdog, and yet be as hard as steel. Whether he's a man of action who does what he does because he needs to be on the go all the time, or whether he really is an idealist who drives himself almost beyond endurance for what he believes is right, I simply don't know. Do you?' Rapp asked, gently.

'Yes,' answered Lois Kenning. 'That is why I love him so.'

Dawlish could not believe his ears, and yet there was no doubt at all of what she had said, in a quiet, husky voice. 'That is why I love him so.' The words hovered in the air, and silence followed, like a sigh. He wished he could push open the door and see her face, but it would be impossible, any sound would be heard and any movement noticed.

Rapp spoke in a voice so soft that it hardly reached Dawlish's ears.

'And why does he love you?'

She said: 'What?' in a tone of surprise, but Rapp did not repeat the question, and she went on, her voice a little stronger but the incredulity quite clear: 'He doesn't even know I exist!'

Rapp said: 'Don't be silly. He's a man.'

'There is just one woman in Patrick Dawlish's life,' said Lois, in a tone of near despair, 'and that's his wife. I don't know whether he sleeps with other women when he's away from home but if he does I'll swear he fantasises that he's with her. When I first met her I couldn't understand it. She isn't – well, she isn't beautiful, and she hasn't got the most seductive figure in the world, but there is some quality about her. I know that now.' Dawlish, his eyes tightly closed, heard every word, even began to understand that she was putting thoughts and feelings into words, emotions which had been bottled up inside. Yet they had only known each other for a few weeks!

Rapp seemed to sense that these words were coming from deep within her, and he did not speak and did not make any sound of movement.

Nor did the detective, on the staircase below.

He could just see the shadowy figure of Dawlish, and guessed he was listening to what was going on in the other room. A faint sound, as of voices, reached his ears; that was all.

Lois Kenning went on in that quiet voice, each word uttered clearly and formed perfectly, almost as if she were repeating a lesson well-learned. In her tone was a tinge of hopelessness, as if her spirit had been crushed.

'I don't know what the quality is,' she said. 'When I first went there I almost hated her because he was hers, and she took that so much for granted, but gradually I came to like her, and – and she didn't take him for granted. She builds her whole life about him, and on making him happy. Inwardly she hates it when he goes away but she sends him off with a kiss and a smile, and I don't think he realizes that she just lives for him to come back. She doesn't let him realize it, that's what is so remarkable.'

For the first time, Rapp said: 'They are a remarkable couple.'

'Oh, yes,' agreed Lois, rather more loudly. 'Remarkable is the one word for them. As for Pat – I don't see how anyone can doubt that he works as he does because he believes in what he's doing. I once told myself he went away so much because he wanted to get away from her, but that was nonsense. She's told me a lot, and I've heard him talking when he's at home. He really hates crime and criminals. *Hates* them both, and fights them because of the harm they do to society. Surely you, a newspaperman, realize that.'

'I'm beginning to,' said Rapp, mildly. 'Certainly I want to; there aren't many people in high places who are not there for what they can get out of it. How long have you been in love with Dawlish?' he asked, without a change of tone.

That was a question Dawlish wanted answered, and he waited even more tensely before she said:

'Six months, I suppose. I didn't really know what had happened to me at first. I used to work at a restaurant – the Big Ben – and he passed the window several times a day. He loves walking. I asked one or two of the customers about him and one was a policeman who told me who he was and where he lived. So I asked in the offices if they had a cleaning job there, and the doorman told me he knew that Mrs. Dawlish had been advertising for weeks for some help in the apartment. So I applied for the job, and she engaged me at once. I told myself that as I came to see more of him I would become disillusioned, but instead – well, I just couldn't help myself. There's nothing I wouldn't do to . . .'

She broke off.

'Get Patrick Dawlish,' Rapp finished for her. 'Is that why you poisoned the chocolates. To get his wife out of the way?'

CHAPTER FOURTEEN

ACCUSATION

THERE was utter silence after Rapp's accusing question. Dawlish could not even hear the others breathing, and was holding his own breath. He did not hear a creak from behind him, but creaks in these old houses were hardly surprising, and it did not occur to him that anyone was on the stairs. In fact Archer's man had moved up two treads, to try to catch what was being said.

Dawlish heard, but Archer's man did not.

'I did not poison the chocolates,' Lois denied in a low-pitched voice.

'Now, come! You want this man for yourself, you saw an easy way . . .'

There was a sharp slap of sound; no doubt she had slapped his face. All Rapp said was 'naughty, naughty', and then he went on: 'Don't get hoity-toity with me, Lois. And don't try that again.'

There was a sudden scuffle, heavy breathing, a stifled exclamation – and Dawlish pushed open the door. He saw the last thing he expected to see: Ed Rapp, reeling away from Lois, staggering helplessly in an effort to keep his balance. She did not move but stood glaring at him, not yet aware that Dawlish was there because Dawlish moved swiftly to one side. Rapp grabbed at the door and saved himself; it was he who was breathing heavily, he who had gasped.

He stood framed in the doorway, as he said in a thin, angry voice: 'Why don't you admit it – you and Dawlish are lovers, and you plotted to get rid of his wife.'

Lois said tensely: 'There isn't a word of truth in it!'

'Not one solitary word,' Dawlish stated, and he stepped forward at last.

Rapp spun round, as if stung. He was a head shorter than Dawlish and had to rear backwards to look up into Dawlish's face. There was fear in the pale eyes behind the glasses. He actually backed a step, but Dawlish stretched out one arm and clutched him by the lapels of his jacket, took a firmer hold and lifted him off the floor.

'What one should do with vermin is tread on them,' he growled.

He peered beyond the helpless man to Lois, whose eyes looked huge, whose body had sagged from the shock of finding him there. He smiled at her, then lifted Rapp higher and turned round and carried him to the banisters.

'Dawlish!' cried Rapp. 'I was only guessing! I only tried to get a story – that's my job!'

'That's right,' Dawlish agreed. 'And you said you came here to help Lois Kenning, remember? And if my memory serves me, to help me too.' He hoisted the man over the railing and held him poised over the stairs. For the first time he saw the detective, who had not had time to get away, being so anxious to hear everything that was said. 'Rapp,' he went on. 'What is your reason for hating me?'

'I don't hate you!'

'Someone with your kind of twisted mind has been sending me and my wife anonymous letters. Is it you?'

'*No!*' cried Rapp. 'Don't – don't let me go, I'll break a leg. Don't let me go.'

'I ought to break your neck,' Dawlish said savagely. 'I wonder whether it *is* you.'

'All I want is a story!' gasped Rapp.

'And you don't care how you get one,' Dawlish rasped. 'Even if you make it up. Well, here is a story for you. My wife was poisoned this morning, and could still die. I, Patrick Dawlish, personally, shall seek out the poisoner and bring him to justice – whether it be you or some other reptile.' He raised the man still higher, and Rapp screamed, then lowered him swiftly but did not let him go until his feet were touching the stairs just above the policeman who was spread-eagled against the wall. 'Catch him,' he added roughly, and the policeman grabbed Rapp as the newspaperman began to fall.

Dawlish turned back to the open door.

Lois still stood in the doorway. The astonishment had faded from her eyes and she was much more herself. He moved towards her, took her arm, and said: 'May I come in?' She led the way into a bed-sittingroom which was pleasantly furnished in bright colours; the bed was in fact a divan. One window faced the back garden, he reasoned. One 'wall' was in fact not a wall but a wooden partition which could be folded back to make this and the front bedroom into one large room – a common feature both up and downstairs in houses of the period.

She raised her arms and poked her fingers through her raven black hair. He was sure that it was a spontaneous and unconsidered gesture but it drew attention to her figure, even to the lovely legs as her dress rose. She did not look away from him as she asked:

'Did you hear what I said?'

'I was just behind Rapp the Rat all the time,' he answered.

'So you heard – everything?'

'Yes, Lois. Every word.'

'I feel so ashamed,' she said.

'Ashamed? What nonsense!'

'It isn't nonsense,' she declared, and she turned and dropped on to two thick cushions, placed on top of each other. He towered over her so much that he sat on one of the only two chairs in the room: a wicker chair which creaked and groaned as he settled into it. 'I should never have come to work for you. I – I don't know what possessed me. I – I'm a married woman,' she stated flatly. 'I couldn't stay with my husband, I left him months ago. I just had to be on my own or else with you. I didn't understand it then and I don't understand it now, but it happened. If only I had stayed away from you I would have got over it.'

'Lois,' Dawlish ordered, 'stop talking for a while.'

She closed her eyes, placing her hands behind her on the cushion, and faced him. For the first time he wondered whether her pose was really unconsidered, for she looked almost as if she were posing for the camera. My, what a figure she had! She was as beautiful a woman as he had ever seen, with flawless features; an Italian beauty at its most superb. And she had left her husband for him! It made no sense.

When she opened her eyes, they were huge, shiny, fascinating.

'I'm sorry,' she said. 'I'm truly sorry.'

'Lois,' he said in turn, 'you do know you are under suspicion of putting the poison in these chocolates, don't you?'

'Yes,' she replied.

He made himself ask: 'Did you?'

She half-closed her eyes again; it gave her the look of a siren, and she whispered huskily:

'No.'

'The police may try to prove that you did.'

'They can't prove what isn't true.'

'No,' agreed Dawlish. 'They can make things damned uncomfortable while they're trying, though.'

'I – know.'

'Have you told the police the whole truth?'

'Yes. Everything.'

'When they questioned you at my apartment was everything you said true – such as, did Felicity ask you to get the chocolates for her?'

'Please,' said Lois, pleadingly, 'don't you doubt me!'

'Please,' he said, gently, 'answer me. Did she ask you to get the chocolates for her?'

'Yes,' answered Lois, her voice barely audible. 'She did. She even offered to give me the money but I said I'd put it on the shopping bill.'

'Good,' he said. 'That's *very* good.'

'Why?'

'Felicity will be able to confirm it,' Dawlish told her. 'She is improving, thank God. And if there is corroborating proof of one of the things you've said it makes the other statements seem more likely to be true.'

'Mr. Dawlish,' she said, with great simplicity, 'I have not lied.'

'Lois,' he said, 'I don't think you have.'

'But I could have put the arsenic into the chocolates, even if Mrs. Dawlish did ask me to get them.'

'Yes,' he agreed. 'You aren't out of the wood yet, but...'

'It doesn't seem to matter,' she interrupted, hopelessly.

'Don't be silly,' he rebuked sharply. 'It could make a lot of difference to your future.'

'Just at the moment nothing matters,' Lois insisted. 'While I kept this to myself, while I worked at the penthouse and saw you sometimes there was a lot to live for, but now you know – I tell you, I feel ashamed beyond words.'

He did not speak.

She shifted the position of her arms, and sat with her hands clasped lightly in front of her. She looked so young and helpless. He reminded himself again that this might be a deliberate pose to win his sympathy but nevertheless she was so lovely and forlorn and his natural instinct was to want to help her.

'Lois,' he said, 'you don't have to be ashamed of being in love.'

She didn't respond.

'And I don't have to return that love to feel very proud you feel so deeply,' he went on. 'Especially when a woman as beautiful as you is involved. Don't feel the least bit ashamed, Lois. I hate to think you do. Felicity would hate it, too.'

She still didn't answer, but she began to cry.

She cried silently, and he remembered the period of silence when Rapp had been with her; then she had cried without making sound. Her shoulders shook and she cupped her face in her hands. She looked – adorable. She looked – a picture of pathos. The temptation to move forward, to put an arm about her shoulders to comfort her, was almost irresistible. But there was a cold streak of common sense in him. If he did that, if he went even part of the way towards soothing her physically, there was a great danger that she would read more into it than there was.

Too much.

So he sat back in the chair, feeling a brute and letting her cry. Soon, he would have to interrupt or to stop her; soon, he would have to go. For the first time he realized that his coming here and his staying with her alone could be misunderstood. Even at that stage he would probably not have seen the possibilities so clearly but for Rapp's innuendo.

What the newspaperman thought, the police might think.

My God, so they might!

He had known they were outside, he hadn't sneaked in, but – they were hard realists. They had even stationed a man on the stairs after his arrival, and they were doubtless questioning Edgar Rapp at this moment. A cloud of doubts and apprehensions thickened over him, but through it there was this woman, still crying but less bitterly.

'Lois,' he said, 'I will do all I can to help, and . . .'

The door burst open.

Two men were there, one of them with a camera and

flashlight; the camera flashed half-a-dozen times. Then a man said in a gruff voice: 'Get out of it, you devils!' and the two men, one of them Rapp, disappeared. Now there were three policemen, all big men, but Archer wasn't among them. The biggest had iron-grey hair, a florid face, a pair of deep-set, unwinking eyes.

'Pat!' Lois exclaimed.

'Sorry about this, sir,' the grey-haired man said. 'I was coming to see this lady and those newspapermen sneaked in ahead of me. What they won't do to get a picture!' He sounded shocked but Dawlish had no doubt at all that the entry had been carefully planned in advance, in the hope of getting a photograph of him and Lois in some kind of compromising situation. Well, that hope at least was dashed.

'Who are you?' asked Dawlish.

'Detective Sergeant Snow, sir – South West Division.' The big man showed his card, already in his hand. 'I have a warrant to search these premises, and came for that purpose.

'To *search*!' Lois exclaimed.

'Yes, madam.' Snow was studiously polite. 'I hope I haven't come at an inconvenient time for you, sir.'

'No,' Dawlish said. 'It makes no difference to me.' The last thing he must do was to explain his presence, all policemen were trained to see voluntary explanations as half-truths. 'Presumably this is about the poisoning of my wife.'

'Yes, sir.'

'I see.' Dawlish turned to look at Lois, who was no longer crying but so obviously had been; her eyes were very red and puffy. 'Lois, I'm extremely sorry about this but the police have to check every possibility. I imagine since I'm here unofficially, they would like to search me before I leave.'

Snow was taken aback.

'That won't be necessary, sir . . .'

'I think it is,' Dawlish said. 'We can use the landing or the hallway.' He put a hand on Lois's shoulder and squeezed, felt her trembling, felt her eyes on him. 'I will do all I can to help,' he said again, 'and I'm sure Felicity will, too.'

He turned as if he were betraying Lois Kenning, which was an idiotic thought.

Despite the fact that he had demurred, Snow made a thorough search of Dawlish's clothes, checking all the linings and even the shoes and his tie for any hiding place where arsenic might be found. This was done on the landing, while two men and a woman officer searched Lois's room, and the baby cried intermittently in the flat above. At last the job was done, and Snow said:

'Very grateful for your co-operation, sir.'

'I think you've overlooked one thing,' Dawlish said. 'I am even more anxious to find out who poisoned my wife than you are.'

Snow managed to say: 'I'm sure you are, sir.'

Dawlish walked round to his car, much more slowly than he had come away from it. He had now no doubt at all what was in the minds of the police, no doubt that the possibility of this being a plot between lovers to murder an unwanted wife had occurred to Rapp when they had been talking in his, Dawlish's, apartment. That explained his sudden change of manner and his rush to get to this place.

Dawlish pulled out of the parking spot, and drove back across Battersea Bridge and direct to the Westminster Hospital. There were practically no formalities, and a night sister took him to the ward, shared by three people, where Felicity lay unconscious, under sedation. He had never seen her look more pale or more fragile. He stood looking down for several minutes, then turned to the night sister.

'Is the danger past?'

'We think so, Mr. Dawlish. We've certainly no reason to think otherwise.'

Dawlish nodded, and turned away.

Coming here he had not been aware of the curiously aseptic odour, the unnatural air of cleanliness, the beds visible through open doors of the general wards, but he was acutely aware of them as he went back. The night air outside was cold and there was a spit of rain he hadn't noticed before. He stood by the side of the car, unseeing but for the image of Felicity's face. There was no doubt now; no reasonable doubt that she would be all right.

This time.

And he was all right: still unharmed, not even attacked.

But would whoever had poisoned her try again?

And was the danger to him more acute, not less? The first

attack had been on Felicity so there was not the slightest doubt of the seriousness of the threat. An attack could come at any moment, out of the darkness: *now*.

Nearby, he saw a shadowy movement.

Nearby, he heard a click of sound, which could be the cocking of a revolver. He had heard such a sound a thousand times and the instinct to duck under cover was so strong that he dropped down.

On that instant he heard a zutt of sound; saw a flash; and heard a bullet strike the metal of the roof of Felicity's car.

CHAPTER FIFTEEN

ATTACK

As Dawlish dropped, as the other sounds came after the flash of the shot, he gasped loud enough to be heard. There followed a few seconds of intense stillness and a noise only of distant cars. Next, he heard a creak and a slither; what might be footsteps. The shot had been fired from behind him, from a spot where many cars were parked; in his mind's eye he could see the reflection of the flash on a dozen shiny roofs. He was squatting. His gasp may have made his assailant believe that he was hit but there was no certainty that the other was fooled. He moved so that he was in better control of himself. If he showed his head above the roof of the car the man might shoot again, but if he peered from behind the cars he might not be seen.

He felt very calm; at its beginning, physical danger always affected him like this.

He peered along the lane between two rows of parked cars.

Not thirty feet away was another, small man, crouching, pointing. Dawlish darted back, there was another *flash-zutt-bang* and on the instant a familiar voice came from somewhere nearby:

'There he is!'

That was Edgar Rapp.

Another man shouted, another shot cracked, a much more vivid flash lit up the cars from the flashlight of a camera. Footsteps sounded. Dawlish saw one man run away from the place where he had been crouching, then a second. The first turned and fired again but Dawlish felt nothing. He drew in a deep breath as he leapt towards these men. Another, the third, who was coming from between two cars, banged into him. Dawlish reeled away one way, the third man another, while the first two raced on. One of them turned and fired, and a fourth shot cracked loud in the quiet.

'Sorry,' gasped the man who had banged into Dawlish. Then in a tone of alarm he added: 'He's got Ed!'

Understanding came swiftly to Dawlish.

Two men had been down here waiting to shoot him while Rapp and his cameraman had been here to see what happened. Once the shooting had started they had shown themselves, ignoring the risk of being shot, and the reporter had been hit.

A motor-cycle engine roared.

The photographer had now reached Rapp, who was bending down and pulling up his right trouser leg. A man came hurrying from a bunch of cars and a voice sounded clearly: 'That was shooting.'

'Ed, where did they get you?' the photographer demanded in shrill alarm.

'He didn't get me anywhere,' replied Rapp with disgust. 'I caught my shin a hell of a wallop on a bumper. Look at the bloody thing!'

He was being absolutely literal, for a narrow stream of blood was flowing from a gash in his leg, on one side of the shin. He must have dodged in a reflex action when the attacker turned, and caught his leg: few blows could be more painful. In spite of it, he held his head up and listened as the motor-cycle engine faded into the distance; then he looked at Dawlish and said in his high-pitched voice:

'Well, you were lucky.'

Then two more men arrived, one of them a doctor, and someone said they must send for the police while another said they should take Rapp to the Casualty Department which was just round the corner. Dawlish knew exactly what the pattern of events would be: questions, a search for bullets and for empty shells, more questions – it would be interminable. And if the police really wanted to question him they knew where to find him. While men were talking, some marvelling and others shocked, and while a crowd gathered, Dawlish slipped away.

The rain was slightly heavier but the walk would do him no harm and he was tired of being interviewed; of talking at all. He needed a period of peace and quiet, and would be better off at home than here.

Would he, though?

He would be much better off at his club, the Carilon,

which was in a terrace behind the Mall. It was a longer walk than he really wanted but once there he could have a steak and all he needed to eat, and some beer, and freedom from questions, for no one would interrupt him in the dining-room or grill-room. Even if the police came they would be politely told that he hadn't yet arrived. He glanced over his shoulder and saw a taxi with its *For Hire* sign alight, and a few minutes later stepped into his club.

'If Mr. Childs or anyone from my own branch calls I'll talk to them,' he told the head porter, who had a kind of telepathic communion with the club's telephone operator. 'Otherwise, I'm not here until I send you a message.'

The head porter was tall, thin, cadaverous-looking; not unlike Lane.

'Very well, sir,' he said.

Few members were in the grill-room, a section of the club still sacrosanct for members only, which – among other things – meant no women guests. Most were behind news-papers or poring over books. Dawlish went to the grill counter where flames were leaping and fat spitting on a steel grill over a charcoal fire. He selected a large, chunky rump steak and two sausages, tomatoes and chips, which were still called chips and not French fried potatoes at the Carilon. When he reached his corner table a silver tankard of his favourite 3-X beer was already waiting, with a copy of the *Evening Standard*. No one spoke. He drank, skimmed, read more closely a short paragraph on the back page about the wife of Mr. Patrick Dawlish, the Deputy Assistant Com-missioner for Crime, being taken to hospital. Whoever had told the story had been very cautious.

His steak came, medium well done; luscious.

When he had finished that he took a large wedge of apple pie from the sweets trolley, and some thick fresh cream. None of the excellent food he had eaten in Switzerland came up to any of this, and he lingered over it. Not until a pot of coffee and a smaller one of cream was on his table did he send a message to the head porter. A message returned at once.

'A Mr. Rapp of the *Daily Globe* is in the lobby, sir. He has been waiting for twenty minutes.'

Dawlish allowed him to wait for another five minutes before going along. Rapp was in a small room off the main lobby, reserved for members with guests. He was reading the *ABC*, as if trains going from anywhere in England to anywhere in England were of absorbing interest. He was probably aware that Dawlish was in front of him, but did not put the book aside until Dawlish said:

'Whatever else you lack, it isn't nerve.'

Slowly, Rapp put the book down on a small table by the side of his leather armchair. He looked up. He was pale, and there was a drawn expression at his eyes and forehead which suggested he was in some pain. Dawlish saw a tiny chip off the right lens of his glasses, and a scratch on his forehead which had been dabbed with some kind of antiseptic, a few strands of cotton wool still adhered to the roughened flesh.

'I know you probably won't believe me but we have something else in common,' Rapp retorted. 'A lust for the truth.'

'The ways of getting it being unimportant,' said Dawlish.

'The ends justify the means in my book,' said Rapp. 'And from what I know of some of the things you've done to solve cases, you aren't too particular about what means you take, sometimes.'

Dawlish felt his jaw champing, but managed to say: 'I'll grant you that.'

'Dawlish,' Rapp asked in a tense way, 'let me ask you a question. Do you trust Lois Kenning?'

'I trust everyone until I've reason not to.'

'And you don't consider you've reason?'

'Not yet.'

'My God!' breathed Rapp. 'A romanticist!'

'Never mind the commentary,' Dawlish said roughly. 'Do you know she was involved in the attempt to kill my wife?'

Rapp said slowly: 'No, I don't. No, I don't *know*. But I think she had a damned powerful motive. I think she thinks that if your wife weren't in the way, she could put you in her pocket.'

Dawlish said stonily: 'Do you?'

'Any woman would agree with me,' Rapp said, testily, but he didn't dwell on the angle, simply went on: 'I know something else.'

'What?'

'Archer and Snow believe you two were in it together, that it's a "get the wife out of the way" crime,' Rapp told him. 'If I'm sorry about anything I've done today, it's not trying to crack Lois Kenning, and it's not telling you half-truths. But if I hadn't gone straight from your flat to her place you wouldn't have gone there, would you? You followed me and found yourself there.'

'That's right,' Dawlish agreed.

'Well, the police don't believe it. I heard enough backchat to know they think you've often been to her place, and went tonight of your own accord. Ever been there before?' he asked sharply, almost waspishly.

'No.'

'I hope to God you can prove it,' breathed Ed Rapp.

That sounded as if the wish came from the heart; and he also seemed to doubt whether Dawlish could prove what he had just said. Standing in the small room with the high ceiling, Dawlish felt a chill run through his veins, for nothing could have made him more certain that Archer seriously suspected him. He moved from where he was standing and sat in a huge armchair; all the chairs in the Carilon had been made on the assumption that every member would be a mammoth. If Rapp knew he had dropped into the chair because his legs felt weak, the man showed no indication.

Dawlish made himself ask: 'Do you know if they found anything significant in Lois Kenning's room?'

'I had to choose between staying there and following you, and I chose to follow you,' answered Rapp. 'Soon after Chilli and I got to the hospital – he's the photographer – we noticed a chap skulking around, that's how we came to be where we were. I know I could have shouted a warning,' the newspaperman went on, 'but Chilli wanted an action pic and I thought the swab would leap at you with a hammer or some such, I didn't expect him to use a gun. I can ring my office – they'll probably know whether anything was found or Lois Kenning was clean. Is there a callbox here?'

'Yes,' Dawlish said. 'I'll show you.'

He crossed the main hall of the club, known affectionately among members as the mausoleum, to a recess where two public telephones stood beneath new-looking metal hoods; both were deserted. He was tempted to wait, but he did not want the newspaperman to think that he was too anxious to hear the result of the call. Yet he was anxious. He simply could not bring himself to believe that Lois Kenning was involved in an attempt on Felicity's life.

He went over what she had said to Rapp, and most of it came back clearly; he doubted whether he had forgotten much. In some ways the details were of vital importance but of greatest significance was the fact that she loved him.

Fact?

Of course it was fact, much more than a claim.

He remembered a case which he had investigated years ago involving a youth who had fallen helplessly in love with a married woman. He had kept this to himself for years allowing the love to grow and grow until it had become more than an obsession, a deadly cancer in his mind. Lois reminded him vividly of that. And he had not suspected how she felt for one moment.

Had Felicity?

If she had, it would be like her to say nothing to him; to let Lois work at the flat, to – worship. Worship! What the hell was he thinking about to let himself use that word? It was crazy! The whole situation was crazy, and yet if she had told the truth Lois had been prepared to sacrifice everything for a dream; for a love which would never, could never be returned.

Or was Rapp right?

Did she think that if she did not have Felicity to compete with, she could have 'won' him?

Oh, lord! How crazy could one get? He had to force his thought into other channels, and there was plenty to think about. More than plenty. There was the whole future of his branch of the C.I.D., his own personal future and the future of the International Police Conference. How vital those had seemed that morning; and how trifling, or at least how easily forgotten, when Felicity's life had been at stake.

The man with the toneless voice really meant business, but now another element had been introduced. *Two* men had been involved in the attempt to shoot him.

His thoughts were interrupted when he saw Rapp move back from his telephone booth, put down the receiver, and turn round. It was impossible to judge his feelings from his expression, but he limped badly, and the little break in the lens gave off scintillas of light.

At the same moment the footsteps of several men sounded in the main lobby and he judged them to be of big and heavy men. He felt almost certain that they were policemen and had no doubt at all that they had come here to see him. The head porter asked with querulous courtesy:

'Can I help you, gentlemen?'

'Is Mr. Dawlish here, please – Mr. Patrick Dawlish?'

'I'll find out for you, sir,' the porter said, as if he really wasn't sure. 'May I have your name, sir?'

'I am Chief Inspector Archer of New Scotland Yard,' Archer announced.

'If you will please wait here, sir.' The porter obviously indicated chairs, and then his footsteps sounded; in a moment he would ask Dawlish by dumb-show whether he was in or not. There was no point in refusing to see Archer but why had he come here with several men?'

Rapp was now by his side.

'They took Lois away,' he whispered. 'I don't know what they found but they certainly found something or they wouldn't have taken her to the Yard. Officially she's helping the police, but we all know that's a police preliminary to making a charge.'

Rapp stopped, and he sounded breathless; much as he had been when a short while before he had breathed: 'I hope to God you can prove it.'

CHAPTER SIXTEEN

INVASION

RAPP's voice faded; and Rapp moved away.

Dawlish saw Archer glaring at the reporter and sensed that Rapp had made himself as unpopular with the police as he had with him, Dawlish. The strange thing was that Dawlish was thinking of the police as something separate and apart from him; no longer regarding himself as one of them. That was how strange a barrier had been built between them by events in a matter of a few hours.

In a way, this visit made the barrier seem stronger, for it was unquestionably an invasion of privacy. No, he thought bleakly as he returned Archer's stare: an invasion of sanctuary. An Englishman's home might be his castle, but the club of a certain class of Englishman was a citadel. One man coming here to question him would not have been important, but there were three. Yes, invasion was the only word. And Archer had moved simultaneously with the head porter, as if intent on crowding him, perhaps on antagonizing Dawlish.

Nonsense!

But was it?

Rapp had slipped away, Dawlish was now near the main lobby with Archer facing him and the head porter alongside Archer, who said with scathing emphasis.'

'Are you at home to this gentleman, sir?'

'Yes,' Dawlish answered, brusquely. 'Is there a Members' Room vacant?'

'Several, Sir.'

'I'd like Number 4, if it's available.'

'It is, sir,' the head porter told him.

The Members' Rooms were on the far side of the lobby, small rooms where members could interview or be interviewed in complete privacy, a great boon especially for out-of-town members. The head porter led the way, Dawlish followed, and the head porter opened a tall, dark oak door on to a room with a circular table, club chairs, all that was necessary for comfort. And there were four chairs. Dawlish indicated them with a sweep of his right arm as the head porter closed the door. The light was from lamps fastened to walls panelled in light coloured oak.

'Well?' Dawlish asked, abruptly.

'Mr. Dawlish, sir,' said Archer, 'I am in a very difficult position.'

'Why?'

'It is my duty to ask you certain questions, but as you are my superior in the force . . .'

'That makes no difference at all,' Dawlish said. He was glad beyond words that Rapp had made the police attitude very clear and that nothing of this really took him by surprise. Over-affability would do more harm than good, while hostility or refusal to co-operate would do even more harm. 'I am quite prepared to answer any questions.' He saw one of the others take out a pocket tape recorder, and glanced towards it. 'I've no objections to the questions and answers being recorded, on the understanding that there is no cutting or editing done on the tape.'

Archer said with obvious relief: 'That's all right, it won't be touched, sir.' There was a click as the tape recorder went into action and almost before Dawlish realized that, Archer asked a question which took him by surprise. 'Why did you run away from the parking area at the Westminster Hospital just now?'

'I wouldn't say "run away",' replied Dawlish. 'I was famished and I knew that if I waited until you or your men arrived it would be hours before I ate. So I made sure you had been called, then took the first available taxi here.'

'Leaving your own car behind.'

'Not mine – my wife's. And yes: it has a bullet hole in the roof and was a piece of evidence I wouldn't, as a policeman, want to see removed. Did you catch my assailant?'

'No, sir.'

'Have you . . .' began Dawlish, and then he almost choked with a sweeping fear of a danger he had not thought of before. A danger to Felicity. What the hell was the matter with him? He drew in a deep breath and went on: 'Have you made sure my wife is protected?'

'Absolutely sure,' Archer said with great emphasis.

Dawlish said heavily: 'Thank you.' He waited again but was still shaken by his own oversight. Of course there was a policewoman in the ward with Felicity, one would be there to take a statement whenever she came round; but instead of leaving the car park after the shooting he should have gone straight back to the ward and made sure of the position. Archer, if he were half a policeman, would wonder why, if he'd had any doubts, he hadn't made sure.

'Mr. Dawlish,' Archer asked, 'how often have you visited the woman Kenning at her home?'

'Never,' Dawlish said. 'Never before tonight, when I followed Rapp.'

Archer's voice held an incredulous note: 'Never, sir?'

'Never.'

'On what terms are you and the – and Mrs. Kenning on, sir?'

'Affable,' answered Dawlish. 'She works for my wife. I know her as a pleasant person who gives my wife a great deal of domestic satisfaction. I don't know her well,' he added. 'I'm away as often as not, and even when I'm in London I usually start for the office before she arrives.'

'I see, sir.' Archer's voice was loaded with scepticism.

'Why do you doubt what I say?' Dawlish asked, forcing his voice to a pleasant pitch as if he were amused rather than angry.

Archer hesitated and Dawlish waited. The tape recorder made a faint whirring sound and one of the other men's breathing was stertorous, as if he were asthmatic or else had chronic bronchitis.

Then Archer stated: 'Mrs. Kenning showed considerable affection for you, and great relief when she realized you were safe. I did wonder if that indicated that you were – er – very good friends, sir.'

'I see,' said Dawlish, and he made himself smile again, although inwardly he was raging. Yet Archer was doing a difficult job well; it was the situation which created anger, not Archer's handling of it. 'Shall we look at the implications of what you are saying very straightly, Chief Inspector? You are implying that Mrs. Kenning and I may be lovers and may have conspired together in an attempt to murder my wife.'

Archer gulped several times before he admitted: 'Something like that, sir.'

'There is no truth in the implication,' Dawlish said flatly.

'I am very glad to hear it, sir,' said Archer. 'And your statement will be relayed to the commander first thing in the morning. Perhaps I should add, sir, since you will undoubtedly learn this very soon, that pure arsenic was found in Mrs. Kenning's room – a supply was packed in a small plastic container bag by a firm of industrial chemists; it is used for the manufacture of certain weed-killers. It is sufficient to kill a dozen people at least, over a teaspoonful. Mrs. Kenning denied any knowledge of it, but nevertheless it was there.'

'Oh,' said Dawlish, heavily. He looked levelly at Archer for a few seconds and then went on: 'I am very sorry, and I am very surprised.' Archer's direct gaze met his as he went on: 'Have you searched the kitchen and other premises of the Choc Shop and its staff?'

'Yes,' answered Archer promptly. 'Everyone who could possibly be involved at the place of manufacture has been closely interrogated, and nothing at all suspicious has been found. After all, one would hardly expect to find a *second* supply of arsenic, would one?'

'No, one certainly wouldn't,' Dawlish replied, heavily. After a pause he went on: 'I don't know what else you may want from me, but I'll gladly give you any help I can.' Then he asked: 'Is Mrs. Kenning likely to be charged?'

'That isn't for me to decide, sir,' Archer replied. 'It will be a matter for Mr. Liddell to decide when he knows all the facts.' It was Archer's turn to pause, as if he wanted to allow the words to sink in. Then he went on: 'I don't think I need detain you any longer now, sir. Thank you for your co-operation – and good night.'

He turned and led the others out, the officer who had brought the tape recorder being the last to go, putting the instrument carefully into his side pocket. Dawlish had no doubt that Archer had brought the two men as witnesses; he was not taking the slightest risk of being discredited later. All three moved quickly, and they had left the club when Dawlish reached the main lobby. The porter came from his little cubby hole near the front door, carrying a fold of paper.

'Your earlier visitor asked me to give you this, sir.'

'Thanks.' Dawlish took the fold, and had a momentary flashback to the folded letter which had been his first intimation of trouble. He looked down stonily, half-afraid that he would read five menacing words, but that was nonsense, of course, and all he read was:

> *This time I really must go and write my story. My major question: why should anyone do this to a public hero?*

Dawlish had never felt less like a public hero.

He went out into heavy rain which would have driven him back to the club to call a taxi but for a uniformed policeman who called: 'Your car's here, sir.' And there was Felicity's, close to the entrance. 'Mr. Archer asked me to tell you he's finished with it.'

'Good, thanks,' Dawlish said. The policeman opened the door and Dawlish stooped to get in, but before he was inside the porter came hurrying from the club, calling his name. 'Sorry, I'll be back,' Dawlish said to the policeman and went back. 'What is it, Green?'

'A telephone call, sir.'

'Thanks.' Dawlish brushed rain off his sleeves and shoulders as he went to the telephone standing in the window of the porter's booth. He seemed to have no time to relax, hardly to breathe. He picked up the receiver and said briskly: 'Dawlish.' Although he was now standing still, although he had eaten his meal in peace, he felt as if he were in the middle of some period of perpetual motion, when nothing would stop or allow him to stop.

'Next time I won't miss,' said a man in a toneless voice; and he rang off.

That was the identical moment when Chief Inspector Archer dialled Commander Liddell's number, just after eleven o'clock. Liddell had told him to report back no matter what time the interview with Dawlish finished, and by police standards it wasn't yet late. Liddell, who lived in Islington, was a long time answering but Archer let the call go on and on until at last the ringing tone stopped and Liddell said:

'Liddell.'

'I've just come from Mr. Dawlish, sir.'

'Where are you?' asked Liddell.

'In my office,' Archer answered.

'Have you the tape?'

'Yes, sir.'

'Better bring it to me at once,' ordered the commander. 'Just come yourself.'

It was the first time Archer had been to Liddell's home, a house built only a few years ago on the site of cottages destroyed by bombing. It was roomy and the furniture was contemporary and the hall and rooms where Archer was taken were spick and span. To his surprise, there were beer and sandwiches on a porcelain dish under a matching cover.

'Very kind of you, sir,' said Archer, appreciatively.

'My wife knows what these late jobs are like,' Liddell said. 'Play that recorder back while you're eating.'

Archer placed the little instrument on a nearby table, and switched it on. An armchair which looked spindly and uninviting, proved to be comfortable; Liddell sat on one which was much larger. The conversation began, and Archer ate carefully, the noises he made inside his head drowning some of the sounds. Liddell listened intently, sitting with his fingers pressed together at the tips. The tape ran for about twenty-five minutes, by which time Archer had finished both eating and drinking, and was as absorbed as his chief.

At last, the voices stopped, and Archer switched off.

Liddell pursed his lips for a noticeable time before he asked: 'This habit she has of calling him Pat.'

'It seems very spontaneous, sir.'

'So I gather. What's his manner with her?'

'Wary,' answered Archer.

'Elaborate that,' ordered Liddell.

'Well, I wouldn't like to say this in the witness box,' went on Archer, 'but I get the impression that he's watching himself very carefully, making sure he doesn't say the wrong thing. She is, as well, but she's not so good at it.'

'I see. Have you seen this?' Liddell opened a folder on a table by his chair and took out a photograph. It was of Lois Kenning and Dawlish, the woman on a pouffe or what looked like a pouffe, the man standing and half-turning. It was a good, clear print in glossy black and white. 'Nothing much to suggest they'd been necking there,' Liddell went on.

Archer studied it, and remarked: 'Even her hair's tidy They certainly hadn't been up to anything. But then he knew we were outside. After all, sir, he's got a hell of a lot at stake!'

'So has any man with a charge of murder hanging over his head,' Liddell remarked dryly. 'And the Yard's got plenty at stake, too. What about this shooting?'

'We've found three bullets, all from a .22 Webley, which can kill at close quarters,' answered Archer. 'We did what we could under floodlights and car headlights but the rain's teeming down and we aren't likely to find footprints or tyre-prints. There's no doubt Dawlish was shot at, but — well, sir, I don't want to make it look as if I have it in for him. When this case began I was all for him on the other business, he's done a bloody fine job in my opinion. But he *could* have arranged for a man to shoot at him.' When Liddell didn't answer, he went on: 'I don't say he did, only that he could have.'

'Yes,' replied Liddell at last. 'I suppose he could. What about the motor-cycle?'

'No one seems to have noticed it, and our chaps who had followed Dawlish and were watching his wife's ward didn't pay any attention to the car park. There are a dozen motor-cycles there most of the time, several members of the staff use them.'

'Well, spread the inquiries about it,' Liddell ordered and putting the photograph back in his folder, he added: 'And charge Lois Kenning with attempted murder by administering poison. I was going to wait until we found out where she'd got the arsenic from, but we can get busy on that after the remand.'

'Right, sir!' Archer sprang to his feet. 'Do you want any statement for the Press?' He put the recorder into his pocket.

'Just a simple statement of the charge,' Liddell replied.

He escorted Archer out to the blustery night and saw him get into a car as a driver held open the door. Then he went back to the front room, where they had talked, and glanced through the folder. He stared at the photograph for some time, and then moved across the room to a telephone on a table near the door. He dialled a number with great care, and sat back until a man answered, and he said:

'May I speak with Sir Charles Frazer, please? This is Commander Liddell.'

'Just a moment,' the other said, and his voice seemed to recede and come next from a long way off. 'Uncle! For you.'

Liddell felt strange. This was the first time he had been in direct touch with the Commissioner, for actually the Assistant Commissioner for Crime was the liaison. But the A.C. was on a late holiday and he, Liddell, was doubling the two jobs. Soon, Frazer was on the line, and Liddell announced himself again before adding:

'You asked me to report major developments in the Dawlish case, sir. I hope I'm not too late.'

'No. What has happened?' asked Frazer. Over the telephone he had an aloof way of speaking.

'We've found arsenic in the home of the Kenning woman, sir, and are charging her with attempting to murder Mrs. Dawlish. There are indications but I would not yet say positive evidence that Mr. Dawlish and the Kenning woman are lovers.'

'I see,' said the Commissioner, and he went on without hesitation: 'As I told you earlier, Commander, I want the inquiries pursued with the greatest urgency and thoroughness. If you find evidence against Mr. Dawlish then we shall proceed with a charge. If you don't. I want his innocence made abundantly clear very quickly. This is an extremely delicate affair.'

'So I understand, sir,' Liddell replied. 'We shall leave nothing to chance.'

'Keep me in close touch,' ordered Frazer, and he rang off without saying 'Good-bye'.

CHAPTER SEVENTEEN

WHY?

DAWLISH stepped into his flat, with one question, virtually an obsession, simmering in his mind: *why* was this happening? Why should anyone hate him and Felicity enough to want to kill them? Rapp had asked that and the answer might be significant.

He lay in bed, wondering: *why*?

He woke half-a-dozen times during the lonely night, wondering: *why*?

He woke at half past six, sure that he would not get off to sleep again; and the burden of his question shifted. Did anyone hate him and Felicity enough to kill? Or were they simply working on him, wearing on his nerves, preventing him from concentrating on some vital job in hand?

He had no vital job in hand.

When that thought passed through his mind, he went still, and lay on his back, legs wide apart, hands folded behind his neck, staring at the ceiling: an off-white ceiling without decorations. 'Ceilings,' Felicity had said when they had been decorating, 'were made not to be noticed.' She even liked the lamp and light shade in the ceilings as unobtrusive as could be.

He was not thinking about Felicity.

He was asking himself whether it was true that he had no vital 'job' in hand.

'Job' was such a loose word. What he meant was that he was taking part in no specific investigation except that of the attack on Felicity, which was preoccupying his branch of the Criminal Investigation Department. In fact, however, he was working on the biggest 'job' he had ever attempted: that of helping to forge the International Police Conference into a crime-fighting force such as the world had never seen.

He had been working on this for a long, long time.

In the course of the work he had learned that there were

two kinds of international criminals. The individuals or small groups who took advantage of the ease of transport and communication to go from country to country, to the larger organizations.

The Mafia and others not unlike it.

The drug smuggling rings; the diamond and jewel smuggling rings; the counterfeit money rings.

There were dozens of such groups!

That was not imagination but simple fact: there *were* dozens of such organizations. Some were quite small and operated between only two or three countries; others operated on a world-wide scale and had agents in every large city, had spies and informers in many police forces.

Any one of these might want to bring about the failure of the International Police Conference, and the more powerful ones would work in several ways to ensure that failure. One way was by discrediting police forces. *By discrediting senior police officials* – such as he. And by lobbying, through its influential connections, in the seats of government for support against the financing of the world force.

Was this possibly what was happening; what had caught him in its mesh?

Could he be indulging in a kind of wishful thinking or was he a victim of a deliberate and cleverly organized campaign? And if he was, were there others or had he been selected as the first victim of such a move?

He lay absolutely motionless, only the sheet over him.

He actually said aloud: *'Careful.'*

Because if this were the explanation then it was ten times more dangerous than he had yet realized.

Such an organization as the one he had in mind had in the past lobbied not only governments but newspapers and great industrial corporations. And such an organization could put its hand on not one but a dozen, a *hundred*, motor-cyclist assassins. He felt the icy-coldness which had first chilled his blood melt, and his blood ran warm. He could no longer lie there as if chained to the bed, he had to move about. First he telephoned the hospital, and the report was good; Felicity had slept well and showed still more improvement. Next he went from bedroom to bathroom, shaved, showered, half-dressed, made tea, his mind working at racing speed, testing this possibility in every way he could think of. Wrapped in an old, shabby dressing-gown he went to the kitchen and put on the coffee percolator and began to cook bacon and eggs; four rashers, four eggs, some fried bread, not toast, to absorb what was left of the bacon fat. He did all of these things mechanically yet with intense application.

The first letter had been posted from London just before the conference, so there had been no time for anyone to see how the conference was shaping. But the mood of its members had been known for some time.

There had been nothing at all in the way of threats until then, neither to him nor Felicity; they had talked so freely about the telephone calls and the five-word letters that had there been anything else on her mind, Felicity would have said so.

What other thing was 'coincidental'? He could think of nothing.

What . . .

He cracked eggs into a cup and upturned them into the hot bacon fat, and as they spat and splashed, his mind seemed to stop working; as if he had run up against a brick wall.

What else was 'coincidental'?

Lois Kenning.

She could be deeply involved, but if for the moment he assumed that she was not, someone else could easily have found out that she worked for Felicity; learned that it was her custom to buy those chocolates from that particular shop and take them home and bring them here next morning. So, it was someone familiar with her movements; therefore, someone who watched her closely.

Who could?

Surely, only someone who lived at or near 48 Dander Street, Battersea.

Who else would be so familiar with her comings and goings? Who else might be able to find out that she brought things home and kept them for Felicity overnight? Who else could get into her room, that startlingly colourful and attractive room, and plant arsenic there?

He used a fish-slice to turn the eggs, then to lift out the bacon and put it with the eggs on a plate, poured out the fat and finished frying the bread in a dry pan. As he put the laden plate on a tray, he side-swiped salt and pepper, bread, butter and marmalade next to it and carried everything into the big room, putting the tray on the table by the corner windows. The rain had stopped but heavy clouds scudded across the sky and the sun shone fierce but fitfully over the river and the buildings. He ate with tremendous gusto, the new thoughts still flashing in and out of his mind.

All of these last things depended on one vital factor: Lois's innocence.

If she were guilty . . .

That would make no difference to the main theory: if she were guilty and in the direct pay of someone else, then only a shift of emphasis was needed. Everything else would fit in. It was hard to believe in view of her behaviour that she was not as much in love with him as she declared, that she was acting that part, but even if she were employed by the Farenza – a kind of Mafia – that did not mean she could not fall in love with him. A woman set to spy on him had, once before. In fact it could more easily explain the desperation in her manner; the fact that she had seemed to be unable to control her emotions. Whatever the truth about Lois, the possibility that this was a deliberate effort to prevent him from strengthening the International Police Conference remained, but . . .

How could he prove it?

If he were the only one who was under attack, the only way would be to catch some of the attackers, but they may not know much; men and women employed by the Farenza often did not know why they were assigned to this job or that: they simply carried out their instructions without knowing why. But if this were an attempt to weaken the conference, it would surely not be confined to discrediting or distracting him. Others were virtually certain to be under attack.

As he thought that, he also thought: but they may tackle us one at a time.

He mopped up the savoury-tasting fat with a piece of bread which was getting stale, then went into the kitchen for coffee. It was now nearly a quarter to eight. Within half an hour his oldest associate, van Woelden of Amsterdam, would be at his office, and he might be there already. Most of the European policemen started early, just as European shops and factories opened earlier than the English.

There was van Woelden; and there was Randy Patton, in New York.

What time was it in New York? He always had to work it out. They were five hours ahead – or was it behind London? Ahead. No, behind. So it was now in the early hours in New York, about two or three o'clock. He knew Patton's number at police headquarters, where he held a position similar to Dawlish's in London but could never remember his private number. He took a cup of coffee to his desk and opened his address book. There it was: Riverside 8–12312. As he dialled the operator it flashed through his mind that the telephone might be tapped; if a man in a privileged position were under suspicion wire-tapping could be the only way to find out.

'Operator.'

'Overseas telephones, please.'

'What country, sir?'

'The United States.'

'One moment, sir.'

One moment grew into several, more exasperating because at this time of the day there was little going through to New York. But at last the operator answered in a soft voice which he suspected was Pakistani, and he gave the number.

'Thank you, sir. There is no delay and I shall call you back in a few minutes.'

'Thank you,' Dawlish said.

He went into his bedroom and finished dressing; he had an extension of his private telephone in here, and expected a ring at any moment. He was fully dressed before it came. He strode across the room, his heart thumping: if everything was normal with Randy Patton then his new idea, this new hope, could be dashed.

'Your call to New York, sir.'

'Thank you,' he said, and then heard a deep and familiar voice: Patton's.

His heart thumped so hard that for a moment it was difficult to speak, and Randy Patton said with more than a touch of impatience in his voice:

'Don't fool around. Who's calling?'

'Randy,' Dawlish said, 'how are you?'

There was a split second of silence before Patton exclaimed:

'Pat Dawlish, for heaven's sake! Well, I'm damned, Pat Dawlish!' There was something in his tone of voice which conveyed a message, and the message stilled the beating of Dawlish's heart. 'I can't think of a man I'd rather talk to,' he went on, 'I certainly can't. Are you in New York?'

'No. London.'

'And you've called at this hour?'

'Randy,' Dawlish said, 'listen very carefully. As soon as I returned from Zurich I ran into an awkward problem in London.' If he announced that Felicity had been hurt he would distract Patton so for the moment he let that pass. 'I'm not sure whether it's some maniac who hates policemen generally, or one who has a special hate for me, but I'm under threat.'

'My God!' breathed Patton. 'So am I.'

Dawlish heard every short syllable, knew what they meant; and they were exactly what he had longed to hear; and yet it was almost impossible to believe. He did not answer at once and Patton was so much taken aback that he did not appear to notice the pause.

At last Dawlish asked: 'How, Randy?'

'It's not the easiest situation to explain,' said Patton, 'but – so why not tell you the simple truth? I am under accusation of being the lover of the wife of one of the other police commissioners. There is a lot of circumstantial evidence and three parts of it is false. Sure, I like her well enough, we would get along fine, but she's the wife of an old friend and so far as I'm concerned that's an end to it. But it isn't being allowed to end. The Chief Commissioner and the mayor had anonymous telephone calls about me, the girl's husband had telephone calls and letters. The last I heard he was coming right here to shoot me! It's one hell of a situation, Patrick, and there isn't a thing I can do about it, because . . .'

He broke off.

Dawlish did not speak, although he felt sure that he knew what Patton was going to say. He was quieter than he had been since he had lifted the telephone; more at ease than at any moment since he had returned from Zurich.

Patton went on in an unbelieving voice: 'Most of the others believe it's true. They believe it's true, I tell you. I have to go and see the Commissioner in the morning, and I can tell you now what he's going to ask: he's going to ask me to resign so that there's no risk of a big scandal at police headquarters. And he'll tell me that's what the mayor wants, to get me out of the way so that when the elections come next month he won't have another kind of police scandal to deal with. You want to know something, Pat? I nearly called you, to talk it over. It's a hell of a decision to make and I don't know anyone whose advice I respect more than I do yours.'

Dawlish said gruffly: 'That's a two-way feeling, Randy. Can you hold your breath for a moment?'

'Try me.'

'I am under suspicion of conspiring with another woman to attempt to murder Felicity.'

He stopped. There was no sound except what might be Patton's breathing. The silence went on for a long time and he actually opened his mouth to say: 'Did you hear me?' when Patton breathed:

'That can't be coincidence.'

'No,' agreed Dawlish in a soft voice. 'That can't be co-incidence.'

'Why would anybody ...' Patton began, only to stop. Again Dawlish waited and this time Patton went on more quickly and with a stronger voice: 'Are you beginning to see what I'm beginning to see, Pat?'

'I think so.'

'Discredit a few of us, and the whole conference ...'

'Becomes smeared and discredited,' Dawlish put in.

'And loses some of its strongest supporters,' said Patton. 'My God.'

'Randy,' Dawlish continued with great care, 'there certainly could be others involved. I am going to call van Woelden. Will you call Chick Hargreaves in Toronto?'

'Yes.'

'If either of them has run into trouble then we don't need much more proof,' Dawlish said. 'And if he's in trouble he won't mind being called out of bed.'

'Pat, how are you going to handle this?' Patton demanded.

'You mean, privately or through our offices?'

'Yes.'

'Privately at first, I'd say,' Dawlish said. 'You and I can

release identical statements at the same time.' He gave a choky kind of laugh. 'Can you stall with your chief this morning?'

'If I have to, believe me I can stall,' Patton breathed.

CHAPTER EIGHTEEN

THIRD VICTIM

DAWLISH put down the receiver slowly, and sat very still, looking down at it. He did not doubt the truth now. Who was behind it was a different matter; finding out would be difficult and time-taking, and at the moment was not of prime importance. Proving what was happening to Frazer — through Liddell and Archer — was important. Proving what was happening to the police and the mayor of New York was, too.

The telephone on his desk rang; the one he used for out-going calls and which few others knew. He hesitated. Did the man with the toneless voice know the number? When he answered, was he going to hear something like: 'It won't be long now'? He lifted the receiver and spoke as if he were preoccupied and yet matter-of-fact.

'This is Dawlish.'

'One moment, Mr. Dawlish,' a girl said with a voice carry-ing a heavy accent. 'Mijnheer van Woelden would like to speak with you, please.'

Dawlish's grip tightened. He pushed his chair back and waited; and in his heart had no doubt what this meant. Then he told himself he could be wrong, that this could be a straightforward business call. Could it? So early in the morning? And no — not to this private number. It was un-thinkable.

'Patrick, you are there?' The Dutchman's voice was deep and guttural but did not have the vigour of a few years ago. He was probably fifteen years older than Dawlish, and had been one of the first to serve on the committee which had grown into the International Police Conference.

'Yes, I'm here,' Dawlish said heavily.

'Patrick, I have before me a newspaper from England tell-ing of the poisoning of Felicity. I cannot tell you how deeply grieved I am.'

'You're very thoughtful,' Dawlish replied. He had a moment of disappointment – that the Dutchman had called out of sympathy and not for any significant reason; then he felt angry with himself for such a reaction.

'Is the latest report good?' the Dutchman asked.

'Yes,' Dawlish said. 'She had a good night.'

'I could not be more relieved and at the same time I could not be more distressed,' van Woelden declared. 'And I could not be more concerned on another account. Is it true that you and Felicity had threatening letters?'

'Yes,' Dawlish answered, catching his breath.

'Patrick,' said van Woelden, 'so have I. And so has my granddaughter, Lotte. You remember, perhaps, that I told you she was with child. The child is due in a few weeks' time. She is nervous, who would not be? and she has a history of miscarriages. I am gravely troubled for her. It appears that she had telephone calls and letters while I was in Zurich, and she and her husband did not wish to worry me when I was on such important business. Since I have returned I have been able to think of little else.' His voice rose as he went on: 'And now to learn that much the same has happened to you . . .'

Dawlish said without preamble: 'And to Randy Patton.'

'Randy! Also! It is incredible.'

'Is it?' Dawlish asked.

Van Woelden was slower than he had been with his reactions but he was still quick, and when he uttered a single 'Ach!' Dawlish knew that he had grasped the full significance, and in the next few seconds was considering the implications. The Dutchman's breathing sounded loud and seemed to grow louder; Dawlish had a strange feeling, that someone else was in the room. It was nonsense, of course, yet it was frightening.

The whole situation was frightening.

Randy Patton, van Woelden and he, all faced with acute personal crises the moment they returned from Zurich, all prevented from giving full attention to the urgent task of strengthening the Crime Haters.

'No,' said van Woelden slowly. 'No, it is not incredible. We are to be prevented from making the conference as strong and irreproachable as it must be. Patrick, we must meet, very soon. I will make arrangements for Lotte to be taken to a nursing home and closely guarded, no doubt you are having Felicity protected now, and Randy . . .'

'He is to call me back in an hour or two.'

'He can be here in a few hours,' van Woelden said, 'or you and I can go to New York. Patrick . . .'

'Not just the three of us,' Dawlish interrupted.

'I do not understand you.'

'Not just the three of us,' Dawlish repeated. 'Camilla Felista and the others of the Secretariat are still in Zurich. We need an emergency session and I'll have the notices sent out at once: we need as many delegates as we can get to go back to Zurich . . .' He broke off.

'But the city will be full!' cried the Dutchman. 'The whole city is taken over by the United Nations Conference on Food and Famine, we shall not be able to squeeze in.'

'Then we'll have to have a session for a day only,' Dawlish answered. 'Every newspaper worth its salt and every big radio and television network will be represented. Zurich, tomorrow afternoon,' he went on breathlessly. 'If needs be we'll have to take delegates out to nearby villages or fly them to other cities for the night. What we mustn't do is take any risk with ourselves. If the other side once suspects what we are going to do, they will try to prevent us from appearing.'

'Patrick,' van Woelden said. 'When Randy comes through why not ask him to record a brief statement? I will do the same. And you can, also. If we are prevented from appearing in person – alive – then at least we can explain what has been happening.'

'Yes,' Dawlish said. 'Good idea. We'll do that.'

'Have you any idea of the group who is attempting to discredit us?' van Woelden asked.

'No,' Dawlish answered. 'The only thing I am sure about is that it will be extremely difficult to identify them.'

'The important thing at this stage is to frustrate them,' van Woelden declared. 'If we handle this situation well and can prove to our governments how much the criminal organizations do not want us, then it is reasonable to hope that our governments will see our value and be less cheese-paring in their allotments of money. Patrick, be very careful.'

'You be *very* careful,' Dawlish urged. 'Good-bye.'

He rang off.

He had no doubt at all that he must do what he had planned in those few seconds, but there was one grave danger: that the telephone had been tapped. If by the police it did not matter, but if by 'them' then he could be certain that a concentrated attempt would be made to prevent the emergency conference from taking place. It would not be possible to stop each delegate from leaving, and not practicable to stop the meeting wherever it was to be held.

But it might be possible to prevent the summonses from going out quickly enough: and there was only one place from which they could be sent – the Operations Room at his office. If the conversation had been overheard, then the obvious thing for 'them' to do was to destroy the whole of the communications system: which virtually meant blowing up the whole floor of the 'old' New Scotland Yard and killing everybody in it.

The offices were in desperate need of protection, and a few days ago he could have arranged it with little or no trouble. Instantly.

But would the Yard heed him, now?

If he called Liddell, who was in charge, the commander would take time; in fact he would need more time than there was to spare. Dawlish stood up slowly and deliberately, knowing what he must do: get over to his office.

He was ready to go, had actually opened the door, when the telephone bell rang on his desk.

Someone else was using that emergency line.

He closed the door on a uniformed policeman, and went back, lifting the telephone. This time he was almost sure he would hear that toneless voice, it was wishful thinking to imagine it would be Randy Patton, for instance.

'Dawlish,' he said.

'This is Childs, sir,' Childs said in a calm voice which nevertheless conveyed a sense of urgency. 'I've just had word that some electrical wiring has been found in the hallway here, connected with a charge of dynamite which would blow much of this floor to pieces. This particular device was timed to go off in fifteen minutes, and there is evidence that other bombs are planted here. Three workmen supposed to be checking the supply lines were here two days ago – the probability is that the job was done then.'

After a few seconds in which to digest all this, Dawlish asked: 'How long ago was this found?'

'By now, a minute or two,' answered Childs.

'So we have less than fourteen minutes left,' Dawlish paused only for a fraction of a second, and then went on: 'Tell the staff exactly what has happened. They can go if they want to or they can stay and search. Searching is the only possible hope of saving the communication and operations systems.'

'I'll put it to them,' Childs said.

'I'll be over as fast as a car can get me there,' Dawlish said, and rang off. If both telephones started to ring now they wouldn't make him pause or lose a moment. He strode on to the landing, to see a lift standing open. 'Thanks,' he said to the policeman on duty. 'Are you able to talk to *Information*?'

The man drew a walkie-talkie from a bulging breast pocket of his tunic.

'At once, sir.'

'I'm going to use a police car to get to my office,' Dawlish said. 'Tell *Information* I'd like to talk to Commander Liddell while en route, wherever he is.'

'Very good, sir.' The man was already drawing the antenna out of the socket on the little transistor. 'Any special message, sir?'

'A matter of extreme urgency,' Dawlish said from the lift car as he pressed the 'down' button.

'Right, sir!'

How different speed seemed when measured against need; now, seconds counted, even if everything went like clockwork he would be at his office in less than six minutes, when at most seven would be left to help in the search. He ran out of the lift at the main foyer as a car parked nearby began to move towards him; a policeman with a peaked cap was at the wheel. He got in next to this man, said: 'My office, quick,' and lifted the radio telephone off its hook. Almost at once *Information* asked:

'Mr. Dawlish?'

'Yes.'

'The commander is at his home, sir, standing by.'

'Thanks,' Dawlish said, and paused only for a second or two before saying: 'Commander Liddell?'

'I'm here,' Liddell said laconically.

'I am going straight to my office, which the staff has discovered is planted with a time bomb and indications that others will go off in fifteen minutes,' Dawlish stated flatly. Childs and some staff will stay and search the place – he has already started by now. The chance of finding what we want are negligible but there is another matter with which you can help.'

In a sharper tone of voice, Liddell replied: 'Name it, sir.'

Sir.

'If Lois Kenning didn't poison those chocolates then there's a good possibility that someone with access to her room at 48, Dander Street did,' Dawlish went on, unflurried; he spoke as if the statement were beyond all possible argument. 'Whoever it is might even know where the bombs are hidden at my office. Unless I've been fooled, there isn't much more than ten minutes to go, but if you've a man at Dander Street who can act with speed and authority . . .'

'Archer is there,' interrupted Liddell. 'I'll talk to him straight away.' There was a momentary pause before Liddell added: 'Good luck, sir.'

'Thanks,' Dawlish said, and he rang off slightly easier in his mind. At least Liddell had not jumped to the conclusion that he was raising a scare simply to cause a major distraction.

And Archer was on the job early.

Dawlish put the receiver down. The driver glanced at him without a word but suddenly used his siren and swung into a lane of oncoming traffic, earnest of the fact that he had heard what was said and was swinging into emergency action. Dawlish sat back. There wasn't quite room to stretch his long legs but he was not uncomfortable. He could do no more, and even if the worst happened and he was blown up at the top of the old building, the whole truth would soon be out and he had at least gained a respite for the conference. And the situation had changed completely. The issue was not whether he would die by an assassin's hand nor whether he would be discredited, but whether he would walk straight into disaster.

The car swung round Parliament Square, its siren screeching, swung into Whitehall, then right across a line of traffic and into the old building. One of the women of the night staff was coming out of the lift as he ran towards it and she called in a tone of great distress:

'I wanted to stay but they wouldn't let me!'

'Get as far away as you can,' Dawlish ordered, and added to his driver: 'Make sure no one comes into the building. There should be a cordon stationed round it in a few minutes.'

'I'll do everything I can, sir.'

Dawlish nodded and stepped into the old criss-cross ironwork lift. How it crawled up! He couldn't be sure but doubted whether he had more than five minutes in which to help when he strode into the offices, the doors of which were open. Childs was peering inside the panel of the communications system, and spared only a glance for Dawlish, who sat at his desk and flicked on a switch which would send his words out by teletype machine to every major police force in the world. In a calm voice he said:

'This is Patrick Dawlish of London, announcing an emergency session tomorrow, repeat tomorrow, October 17th at Zurich, for a special report from me and delegates van Woelden and Randy Patton on simultaneous campaigns to discredit us both in our private lives and as the organization's leaders. The attempt is thought to be organized by one or more groups of interests who control criminal activities in various countries. Reports from any other delegates who are suffering from acute pressures to prevent them from concentrating on our special problems should be sent by normal communications channels since this panel from which this announcement is being made is in danger of severe damage if not total destruction. This message is being broadcast by me, Patrick Dawlish, in person.'

He rang off.

He watched Childs straighten up and saw the bleak expression on the older man's face. Childs was as dedicated as he, Dawlish. It was difficult to believe that any minute they might cease to exist as human beings, but no doubt at all Childs believed that was possible.

He said: 'We've found nothing else yet.'

'Well, at least they didn't stop that message from going out,' Dawlish said. 'Where haven't you searched?'

'Your desk,' answered Childs. 'I'll go and examine the

couches and the visitors' table.' He rounded the panel and disappeared from Dawlish's sight, while Dawlish unlocked and pulled open the middle drawer in his desk; all the drawer-locks were controlled by the drawer. Everything was as he would normally leave it; plus pencils, erasers, ink, some scissors, a penknife, some cigarettes and matches all neatly stored in their compartments, Scotch tape, stamps. He pulled the drawer out, that being the only way in which he could easily examine the underpart of the top of the desk.

But he did not remove the drawer altogether.

He stared at a narrow pack of Dari-Golds, soft-centre chocolates which he much preferred to Felicity's rich flavour assortment. He had forgotten these, after Lois had got them for him just before he had gone to Zurich. He felt almost afraid to touch them, although there could be not more than two minutes of a lifetime left if these offices were to blow up.

There might be a only a few seconds.

He took the package out with great care, and placed it on top of the desk, then gripped the lid between the thumb and forefinger of his right hand, and lifted slowly. It came away easily, and that in itself was suspicious, for those lids usually stuck because of the thick padding of the crinkly paper inside. He raised it clear of the box. In the box were six pieces of the chocolate, and on the surface that seemed normal, except that the coating was less shiny than usual, and more even; the surface was usually crinkly, making it more enticing.

He lifted the whole centre of the box and looked underneath. There were tiny wires as there might be in a transistor battery. These were not separate pieces of chocolate but were linked together. Had he taken out one piece – or tried to – he had no doubt that the whole contraption would have blown up in his face.

This was how he was to have been killed.

Was it the explosive which was to destroy the whole of these offices? If so, how would it be detonated?

CHAPTER NINETEEN

HOW LONG?

HE could not be sure of the damage this bomb could do nor of how it would go off, but he felt reasonably sure that they would not have placed more than two bombs here.

He did not know how long he had to work in, and doubted whether Childs did when he called:

'Jim – what time should the balloon go up?'

'We've three minutes,' Childs replied. 'That's according to my stop watch.'

'Three,' Dawlish said in the most casual of voices. 'Isn't there a way up to the roof?' He knew there was, a fire escape route which led from one of the passages, but he wasn't sure which.

'Yes.'

'Will you go ahead and open all doors and hatches?'

Childs appeared at the edge of the control panel, and he could not hide his feelings now – or his consternation, even his fear. But he controlled them as he said:

'Follow me.' He opened the door into the passage and foyer, adding: 'Do you think that's it?'

'It's got wires and things,' Dawlish said, almost inanely.

Childs went to the door marked *Exit*, as he asked: 'How do you think they will set it off?'

'I suppose a simple time contraption.'

'I suppose so.' There was a drab landing with a staircase going up and another going down; the one going up was short, and led to another, narrow door which had an iron bar across like the kind used in theatres and others places where crowds often gathered. On it in black was the word: *Roof* Childs pushed this, and it stuck. He placed both hands on the bar and pushed harder, while Dawlish stood stockstill.

The door jolted open.

'All right,' Dawlish said. 'Thanks. Get the place empty, and warn anyone below there might be a lot of debris flying about.'

Childs made a noise in his throat as Dawlish passed him, holding the roof door open. Beyond were two more steps to the roof level, and chimney stacks, slates, bricks and mortar, and the scudding clouds and the wind. Near him was a small roof garden and some tubs; neglected for years. He carried the box towards it, and as he began to bend down felt an almost irresistible temptation to hurl the box away from him and turn and run. He fought the impulse down, and placed the box on the edge of one of the tubs. Then he straightened up, turned, and ran towards the door through which he had come.

Between him and this open door were two large chimney stacks; suddenly he changed direction and flung himself down between the stacks, flat on his stomach, his face buried in one arm, the other arm covering the back of his head.

Suddenly, there came a roar.

Almost simultaneously a blast lifted him off his stomach and hurled him against one of the chimney stacks. He struck his head. He was aware of devastating noise, as of thunder; of a continuing cascade of bricks and debris. His head felt as if it would burst, he was being shaken up and down as in an earthquake and had no control over his movements; his body was like a jelly. All this seemed to go on for an age, but at last he was aware of a slackening in the shaking and the falling debris, until there were only stillness and silence.

He began to move.

His head still hurt, but at least it was on his shoulders. His arms and legs seemed undamaged, but for rubble which was dislodged as he moved. More fell from his back. He reached his knees, putting out one hand to lean against a chimney stack. He lost his balance, because it wasn't there.

He could see only rubble; bricks, pieces of mortar and stone, pieces of actual chimneys. Dirt. There was a clump of grass. The air about him was full of dust which filled the place where the great chimney stack had been. He turned his head to look for the other stack, but it wasn't there either; just a stump no more than a foot high, jagged at the sides. The whole roof was a mass of rubble. The porch which covered the door leading into the building was gone. Everything was gone.

Except him, Patrick Dawlish!

He got to his feet, staggered, put his hand to his head and

felt the warmth of blood. Gingerly he moved his finger about but he did not think the wound was very serious. He moved laboriously to a pile of bricks and lowered himsel. cautiously. It was useless to try to stand, he simply could no keep his balance. He saw at last, knees on his elbows, staring through the thinning dust towards the thinning clouds. He could hear nothing, and his first conscious thought since the explosion was that the sky was clearing up.

From here, he could see nothing.

But he began to think.

How much damage had been done below – to the com- munications system, for instance? Was Childs all right? Had many people been hurt by falling debris? All of these ques- tions repeated themselves over and over again but he felt no sense of urgency or alarm. Just numbed. Shock, he supposed. How long would he be left up here? It was chilly, whether the weather was improving or not. He actually smiled. After a while he tried to stand up again, and found it much less difficult. Moreover he could see across the river now, to the London County Hall, and on to Westminster Bridge and the Thames.

He saw a movement close by: a man wearing a steel helmet. He felt a moment of alarm before he noticed that the man was standing on a ladder, and realized that these were firemen who had come to his rescue.

He began to laugh.

He could not stop himself until he was by the ladder and stepping down, backwards. The man uttered a few words that seemed stiff and a little absurd, but it didn't matter. What began to matter was finding out what had happened in the offices and below.

When he reached the ground on the embankment itself Childs was with a group of police and newspapermen, and Childs was smiling, not broadly, simply with deep almost painful relief. It was so good to see him. They stood looking at each other while photographers took pictures; and then Dawlish asked slowly:

'Damage in the office?'

'None,' Childs answered.

'*What*?'

'None. The blast went upwards and sideways.'

'Good God!' exclaimed Dawlish. He gulped. 'People?'

'A few minor injuries from falling debris and one or two cars have dents, but nothing serious,' Childs assured him.

'But that's a miracle!'

'Man-made,' Childs declared.

'Man – oh!'

'Can we have a statement, please,' a big man called from the crowd. 'Is it true that Mr. Dawlish found a high explosive in his office, enough to destroy the place, and carried it to the roof where it exploded harmlessly?'

'True,' Childs stated.

'*Did* you, Mr. Dawlish?' From among the crowd Ed Rapp appeared, limping, with his photographer, and his approach appeared to give the others courage; suddenly they were hemmed in by the men from Fleet Street. 'Is that what happened?'

'I suppose it is,' Dawlish admitted.

'You carried an explosive which might have blown you to pieces?'

'Now take it easy,' Dawlish protested. 'If it had gone off while I was in the office it would have blown me to pieces, anyhow. I took a calculated risk, with Childs going ahead and opening doors for me so that I could get the damned thing on to the roof. There appears to have been no serious damage anywhere else. That's enough, I think,' he finished.

'Move away, move away,' a constable urged, and slowly the crowd moved, more flashlights went off, while Rapp with his terrier-like persistence managed to keep close to Dawlish and to fling a question:

Do you know who did this, Mr. Dawlish?'

'Enemies of society, I think,' Dawlish answered clearly. 'Enemies of . . .'

'Organized criminals,' Dawlish continued. 'It is too thorough for the odd individual, and too many men have been involved. Criminals who in all probability have had things too much their own way for far too long, and don't like the signs that the police are really beginning to fight back on an international scale.'

They were now at the foot of the long flight of steps which led up to the main hall, one way by which Dawlish and Childs could get to the office. *An undamaged office.* More policemen were here and it became obvious that the newspapermen were not to be allowed up. Dawlish was conscious of the effort he had to make to talk as he was doing, but he wanted to say a little more, went up several steps and turned to face at least twenty newspapermen, several of them photographers. Childs and a detective sergeant were with him.

Rapp asked: 'Beginning to fight back? Surely the police have been fighting back for centuries.'

'City by city and sometimes nation by nation,' Dawlish said, 'but at least five substantial criminal organizations are international in scope. There isn't yet a single international police alignment against them. The conference is the nearest we've got and it meets only occasionally, has a secretariat with a skeleton staff because there isn't enough money for a full staff, and has to fight red tape and the establishment for every penny it spends. It's time that nonsense stopped. More by accident than design I've become a spokesman for the conference. A few years ago we had a far-sighted Home Secretary who allowed us to build a communications centre here for quick contact with world police forces. There was a plot to kill my wife, another to have me thought guilty of trying to get rid of her. Other conference delegates have had acute problems. Now there has been an attempt to destroy the communications centre here – and it failed by a hair's breadth.'

'Thanks to you,' a man called.

'And we may get the money we need if you chaps can tell the story effectively,' Dawlish said dryly. 'That's all for now.'

He turned and started up the steps, stumbled, and would have fallen but for Childs' support. He went up more slowly, his head swimming, no doubt from delayed shock. He wanted to sit down but had to make himself go on. He felt another man take his right arm so that he had support on both sides, and he both needed it and resented the need. At last they reached the top, and soon a big lift, which would lead to a different landing upstairs. The criss-cross ironwork gates were open and a one-armed attendant stood waiting. Dawlish went in, half-turned to face the gates, and realized for the first time that the other man was Liddell, who must have been among the crowd listening at the foot of the steps.

Childs said with quiet insistence: 'No more talking yet, sir. You need some coffee and a rest.'

'I couldn't agree more.' Liddell was emphatic.

As in a dream Dawlish felt himself supported on either side, out of the lift, round the wide, undamaged passages to his own door, into the room which was blessedly untouched. Instantly the door from the next room opened and a youthfull-looking, handsome man came in with a tray, cream and sugar. This was Gordon Scott.

'Magnificent,' he said simply.

'Put plenty of sugar in that coffee,' ordered Childs, leading Dawlish to an armchair.

'Right!'

Dawlish drank the hot coffee when he sat down, drank a second cup, then leaned back and closed his eyes. He felt someone raise his legs and push a small chair under them, and was much more comfortable. He was aware of voices but not of time. His head ached. He heard men come in, felt one at his head, touching but not hurting; then sponging gently. A faint smell of antiseptic teased his nostrils, and quick as a flash he was with Felicity in that hospital ward.

Sharply, he demanded: 'Is my wife all right?'

'Yes,' answered Liddell from behind him, 'and under strong guard.'

'Thanks,' Dawlish managed to say. 'Thanks.'

He rested there, surprisingly comfortable, until the dizziness and the numbness faded and he knew that he was over the worst; he could begin to think and to talk, now. He shifted his position cautiously, so that he could look round.

Lois Kenning was sitting in a small easy chair, watching him. As she saw him move she jumped up and ran towards him, and before he could speak or fend her off, she was on her knees in front of him, peering up into his face.

And Dawlish wondered with despair: are they *still* trying to trap me? Did Liddell release her so that he could hear me talk to her when he thinks I'm too exhausted to pretend?

CHAPTER TWENTY

FAULT

'PAT,' she said, 'I'm desperately sorry. It was all my fault.'

Fault? he wondered. What did she mean by the word. She was leaning against him and her expression seemed to implore him to believe her – but to believe what?

'Pat,' she said, 'it was my husband.'

'*Hus*band,' he echoed.

'Yes,' she said, and she was nearly distraught. 'I told you I'd left him, I couldn't go on living with him, but I didn't know that before we parted I'd talked about you in my sleep, that he knew why I'd come to work for your wife.'

For the first time, Dawlish allowed himself to take her hands.

'I can't really explain, or rather I can't really expect you to understand,' she went on. 'Everything I told you was true, and yet wasn't the whole truth.' She clutched him more tightly about the legs, and her eyes had the beauty of autumn leaves and her face near perfection. 'You were an obsession with me,' she said, in a strained voice. 'I had never been in love, not really in love before, and – well, I lived in a dream world and you were the centre of it. I used to pretend we were married, I used to lie half-awake at night, my mind filled with fantasies, of you and I living together. Just – living together, laughing, eating, sharing the same couch and the same bed. Pat, it was both wonderful while the fantasy lasted and hideous whenever I came out of it.'

That, at least, he could understand.

'And my husband guessed I was in love, and sometimes heard me call your name, in ecstasy and despair. At one time he had a tremendous admiration for you, but now I know this turned to hate. His mind must have been turned, the David I used to know would never have made those wicked telephone calls or posted letters.'

And that, too, Dawlish could understand.

All this had been happening because of him and he had not dreamed of it. A man in anguish, bitter and vengeful, a woman tormented by unrequited love, and he oblivious. But one man could not have organized these crimes.

She went on: 'Mr. – Mr. Archer talked to him this morning. I was there, that's when I heard all this. My husband was approached by someone – who it was I don't know – to send threats to you and your wife. Then he was fed on lies, that you and I were actual lovers, not just in my fantasies. The more he hated the more ready he was to kill, and the others schemed with him. *He* replaced the chocolates I bought you. *He* put the high explosive in your desk. He hated you so much he didn't care what he did, and he was paid handsomely, too. But basically it was my fault. He is ruined because of me, and I . . .'

'No,' interrupted Dawlish, speaking for the first time.

She looked puzzled. 'But it *was* my fault.'

'You may have sparked the hatred off but the capacity was in him,' Dawlish said. 'Don't torment yourself with self-reproach and guilt.' When she simply buried her face against his knees he placed a hand on her dark hair and stroked, very gently.

And he was aware of her; as a woman, a woman to desire.

They sat like that for a time that seemed long but was measured only in minutes, until Dawlish said:

'I might as well blame myself for being attractive to you. But I don't.'

'Please,' she begged, and looked up at him. 'Don't – don't ever. Pat – you don't hate me, do you?'

'No,' Dawlish said, 'I don't even begin to hate you. I don't even hate your husband, I can imagine a man feeling as deeply about you as you say you do about me.'

'Say?' she echoed, with a touch of bitterness. 'Say! Pat – Felicity could have been killed. And you.'

'Yes,' Dawlish agreed. 'And in New York a policeman who is about my opposite number found himself in a trap nearly as disastrous. That wasn't because of you or because of your husband. Another prominent policeman in Holland was being victimized, too. Don't torment yourself, I tell you, you're not the reason, this isn't your fault. It's the result of the war between society and criminals, and you've helped to bring this to a head because you were used – or your husband was.'

'I don't think any other man would try to soothe me that way,' Lois said. 'Pat – I do love you. It isn't fantasy: I love you absolutely.'

Softly, he said: 'I know.'

'I think I always shall,' she said. 'I really do.'

As softly, he replied: 'I think I hope you do. Or, at least remember.'

'That is beyond all doubt,' she told him. She leaned back, to look at him more intently. He could see the swell of her bosom and the pale softness of her flesh, and the piquant beauty of her face.

He let her stay like that for a while and then eased himself free and to his feet, and with a swift movement placed his hands beneath her elbows and raised her. They stood very close together and he could feel the thumping of her heart. Then he put his lips close to her ear and whispered: 'I wish to God I could let myself feel for you without hurting Felicity.'

She caught her breath.

'You *could* feel for me?'

'Lois,' he said. 'Oh, Lois.'

And then he put one finger beneath her chin and raised her head, kissed her lightly at first and then firmly and then with simulated passion. She clung to him as if to life, but suddenly wrenched herself free and went to the door and fumbled for the handle. 'Please,' she begged, 'don't follow me,' and she went out. He stood with his heart thumping now and his lips burning, and with doubt in his mind: how much of that passion had really been simulated and how much real?

It was so easy to desire: even easy to love.

It was so difficult to be faithful but at those times when temptation was greatest, it was most important to hold fast. A passing fancy mattered little, but a passionate *affaire* ...

He turned to the window, and after a while began to reflect: Liddell must have been convinced about Lois's husband or he would not have let her go. He began to wonder where Liddell was, how long he had been in the armchair with his legs up, half-dozing, perhaps half-conscious. He moved towards the desk and saw Childs sitting at the control panel, obviously taking messages. Childs looked up.

'I'm sorry,' he said. 'I couldn't leave the controls. Replies about the emergency conference have been coming in thick and fast.'

'What do they say?' asked Dawlish.

'We have seventy-one acceptances, three doubtful and one regrets,' answered Childs. 'I . . .' He broke off when one of the black dots on the panel lit up; it was Buenos Aires with a green light. 'Seventy-two acceptances,' he amended. 'I've talked to Camilla Felista in Zurich, and she's come up with a bright idea. There's one of the Lake steamers with plenty of overnight berths and plenty more comfortable deckchairs, not yet put away for the winter. So she's arranged to hire it for twenty-four hours from noon tomorrow. The owners will supply lunch, dinner and breakfast for an all-in fee, much more reasonable than the big hotels.'

'Couldn't be better,' Dawlish said, delighted. 'Camilla Felista is very good.'

'Couldn't be better,' Childs said with a smile. 'I've booked a flight for you by BOAC direct to Zurich, and you need to be at London Airport at ten o'clock tomorrow, so you've the better part of a day to get over this morning's excitements.'

'I think I need it,' Dawlish said ruefully. 'Is there any way of escaping the battery of newspapermen?'

'There's a car waiting for you, and I think Liddell will go with you to your flat,' Childs said. 'Oh – Randy Patton called. He will be in Zurich. So will van Woelden.'

'By the time they get back to their respective homes the heat should be off them,' Dawlish said. He looked very steadily at Childs, and then went on: 'Thank you, Jim.'

'I don't suppose you'll ever realize it,' said Childs, 'but I'll never be able to begin to thank you. Very few people will.' After a pause he went on: 'Including Lois Kenning, who has a sister in Bournemouth and is going to stay with her for a while.'

Dawlish nodded, relieved to know that, and went out and down in the lift with the words ringing in his ears. They were good words to remember, to live with. Already he was feeling much better. The police had cordoned off an area at the foot of the steps, and it was easy to pose for photographs, and then get in the waiting car. He could see someone in the corner but it wasn't until he was inside that he saw that it wasn't Liddell, it was Sir Charles Frazer. Dawlish settled back cautiously, and as the car started off he said lightly:

'All we need now is Sir Arbuthnot Lane to complete the party.'

Frazer looked at him in astonishment, gulped, and asked: 'Do you mean they haven't told you?'

'Told me what?'

'About Lane. He's under arrest, he – good God!' exclaimed Frazer, seeing the astonishment in Dawlish's eyes, 'you *don't* know. He – she – he is Lois Kenning's husband. Kenning is her maiden name. She was only eighteen when they married, ten years ago. He – good lord!' Frazer was almost as baffled as Dawlish. 'I thought you would know. Well. There it is. She told you that her husband was the poisoner, didn't she?'

'She told me everything but his name,' Dawlish said faintly.

'Well, you know his name now. Sir Arbuthnot *David* Lane. And you no doubt see a lot of other things. Why there was so much vindictiveness in his committee's report, and the way he presented it. There is something basically evil in the man, or he would not have let the organization use him so freely. He probably saw himself as a leader of the criminals. He had the tendency to begin with, the jealousy only brought it to the surface. I confess I was not sufficiently detached. I'm sorry. But at least you've the satisfaction of knowing that no one can possibly doubt the need for you Crime Haters now. You will always have my full support, for what it's worth. Well, well! I didn't dream you didn't know. I hope we can work together to dig out the other devils.'

'Closely together,' Dawlish assured him.

Lois's married identity explained so much. And a young woman married to such a man in his late fifties must have almost screamed for romance.

And fantasy.

Well, thank God it was over.

He needed to check with the hospital, take it easy, he might even go to a film or visit friends – anything but work, anyhow. It was still not half-past eleven. He really had the better part of a day before flying to Zurich.

There were the delegates again, in the big dining saloon of the ship.

They were on their feet, cheering and clapping.

They had just listened to messages from a dozen governments, forerunners of many more to come, promising funds.

They had heard van Woelden's story, and Randy Patton's, and had been told by both that the pressure was off. Whoever had tried to strangle the crime conference had not only failed but acknowledged the failure. There was a long, bitter war of attrition ahead but the two sides would start more even. Soon, very soon, they must begin to seek out the men who had actually organized the attempts at sabotage, but not yet.

First, get themselves into a position of strength.

Dawlish saw Camilla Felista at her desk, a rapt expression on her face; she knew they had nothing to worry about for the future. And she saw the newspapermen, squeezed into a bar, Rapp among them. Rapp would always be in the forefront, whatever the story.

The Swiss police were in strength outside.

The Swiss newspapers, like the newspapers of the world, were full of the story of the attack on the 'old' New Scotland Yard and if few knew the distinction between the old and the new, it did not greatly matter. There was acute awareness that what had been attempted once might be tried again, and a shipload of senior police officials must offer an almost irresistible target.

'And we all know that,' Dawlish said, when he stood up to close the special session. 'We also know that whoever organized these attacks must realize that if they kill me, someone will take my place. If by freak of chance they killed all of us, someone would take all our places. As individuals we are vulnerable, but as the representatives of society we are indestructible.

'And we can overcome crime if society will give us the weapons, which means plenty of manpower – which means plenty of money.'

Felicity sat up in bed and watched a televised report of the meeting and watched and listened to her husband. She saw the delight on the faces of so many of his audience, and she felt a deep contentment.

Lois had been to see her.

Now Lois had gone away.

THE END

THE EXECUTIONER: JERSEY GUNS BY DON PENDLETON

THE NAME OF THE GAME WAS BEAT IT! OR SHOULD HAVE BEEN . . .

In the terrorist-infested jungles of Vietnam he had earned himself the title of *Executioner*. And when Mack Bolan left the army to declare his own personal war on America's underworld the title had stuck. From Pittsfield to Miami, Boston to Washington, the Executioner had blasted his enemy out of existence – the lone operator who wreaked untold havoc on the world's most organized crime syndicate – the *Mafia* . . .

The Garden State of New Jersey – a refuse bin for the underworld garbage of New York and Pennsylvania. Bolan hadn't intended it to be anything other than an escape route. But the top Mafiosi, led by the deadly, smiling Mike Talifero, had got wind of his presence in town. They were moving in for the kill. And on that hellish night of nights at the sign of Boots & Bugle, Bolan rewrote his battle plans in letters of blood and flame . . .

0 552 09902 3   40p

CREATED, THE DESTROYER BY RICHARD SAPIR AND WARREN MURPHY

Convicted and condemned to death for a crime he didn't commit. Remo Williams has been resurrected and programmed – not as a normal, functioning human being, but as a cold calculating death machine . . . created to destroy in order to preserve . . . a lethal weapon that has no loyalties, that can only be used in an extreme emergency . . . and aimed with the utmost care.

THE DESTROYER

0 552 09404 8   30p

THE WARY TRANSGRESSOR BY JAMES HADLEY CHASE

He met her when he was down and out – guiding tourists round the
sights of Milan. She was rich, beautiful and self-assured. He was
a down-at-heel drifter on the run from the police. So when she
suggested having lunch with him, David couldn't believe his
luck.

But it wasn't really luck that had arranged their meeting.
It was just a small part of the plan – Laura's plan – in which David
stood to inherit over six thousand lire. All he had to do was help
commit a murder . . .

0 552 09876 0   40p

MAKE THE CORPSE WALK BY JAMES HADLEY CHASE

Money buys everything . . . or at least, that's what eccentric
millionaire Kester Weidmann believed. So when his brother died,
Kester figured all he had to do was buy the services of a voodoo
expert and bring him back to life.

But first he had to find a voodoo expert. And for that he employed Rollo – a small-time operator who used the Gilded Lily
Club as a front. Rollo thought he had it made – it would be the
con trick of the century. But he was reckoning without the inter-
ference of Celie, his smouldering Creole mistress, and Butch, the
club muscle-man, who both decided that Weidmann's fortune
was worth heck of a lot more than Rollo's flabby neck . . .

0 552 09875 2   40p

THE ERECTION SET BY MICKEY SPILLANE

Dogeron Kelly, a walking bomb of a man, suddenly appears in elegant – and not so elegant – New York circles with a suitcase containing a quarter of a million dollars. There are rumours, but no-one is certain where he, or the money, came from. It seems he is out to claim his inheritance – or is there something else he is after?

Sharon Cass, for instance, a bright and beautiful girl with some very special gifts for the right man?

Whatever it is, Dog Kelly isn't telling, but his search takes in a baronial old-family manor; the high levels of international illegal traffic; paid mobsters; the rich and the famous ...

THE ERECTION SET

Another blockbuster by one of the world's most popular writers.

0 552 09111 1   40p

PANDORA'S BOX BY THOMAS CHASTAIN

Take a black, Ivy League-educated, unemployed Vietnam veteran – a criminal who's a connoisseur of beautiful women and fine art ...

Pit him against a New York Police Inspector – a bloodhound who doesn't believe in unsolved cases ...

In a multimillion dollar heist involving the ransom of six priceless paintings from the Metropolitan Museum of Art ...

And you've got ...
Operation
PANDORA'S BOX

0 552 09865 5   50p

A SELECTED LIST OF CRIME STORIES THAT APPEAR IN CORGI

All these books are available at your bookshop or newsagent: or can be ordered direct from the publisher. Just tick the titles you want and fill in the form below.

CORGI BOOKS, Cash Sales Department, P.O. Box 11, Falmouth, Cornwall.

Please send cheque or postal order, no currency.
U.K. send 18p for first book plus 8p per copy for each additional book ordered to a maximum charge of 66p to cover the cost of postage and packing.
B.F.P.O. and Eire allow 18p for first book plus 8p per copy for the next 6 books, thereafter 3p per book.

NAME (Block letters) ....

ADDRESS ....

(JUNE 76) ....

While every effort is made to keep prices low, it is sometimes necessary to increase prices at short notice. Corgi Books reserve the right to show new retail prices on covers which may differ from those previously advertised in the text or elsewhere.